THE CATS' LAIR

THE CATS' LAIR

C. H. Foertmeyer

Writers Club Press
San Jose New York Lincoln Shanghai

The Cats' Lair

Writers Club Press
an imprint of iUniverse, Inc.

For information address:
iUniverse, Inc.
5220 S. 16th St., Suite 200
Lincoln, NE 68512
www.iuniverse.com

ISBN: 0-595-23778-9

Printed in the United States of America

For my mother—for her never ending love and devotion.

What sometimes seems merely strange and out of the ordinary may be much more. There are worlds parallel to our own of which we have no knowledge or any idea of their existence.

Contents

Acknowledgements

It is with great appreciation that I acknowledge my brother, Tom Foertmeyer, for his great help in the editing of this work and the designing of the front cover. His interest in my projects is very gratifying and appreciated.

Many thanks to Digital West Media, Inc. of San Diego, California DBA DesertUSA.com for permission to use the bobcat photo my brother designed into the image seen on the front cover of *The Cats' Lair*.

Foreword

The characters described in *The Cats' Lair*, with the exception of the Father, and possibly the Guardians, are fictitious. The locations in *The Cats' Lair* are also fictitious, but again, with the possible exception of Father Mountain. I'll leave that for you to decide.

As to the concept of time put forth in *The Cats' Lair*—maybe? How else do you explain the phenomena of walking into your living room and—for a brief, extremely brief moment—seeing a person standing in the corner? Where do they come from? Where do they go? The answer: They live there—with you. There is only one world, but there are many time rings within it, concentric rings, converging on the beginning of time. You walked into the room and for some unexplained reason your vision penetrated one of the many barriers separating one time from another and focused in the next ring. There, before you, ever so briefly, was a *former* occupant.

Proof? There is none—yet. Do I believe it—perhaps? Does anyone believe it?—Big Red and Little Jimbo do. Ask them.

C.H. Foertmeyer

CHAPTER 1

The Map

*A*t Six o'clock Sunday morning, July 7, 2002, Jim Preston stared out his bedroom window to the street below. The streetlights still burned as the early morning sky had turned a deep royal blue and Rockaway, for the most part, still slept beneath it. Anxious for morning to arrive, sleep had eluded Jim for most of the night. *Today was the day.*

Jim had spent the entire day, Saturday, making the final preparations for his trip to the Colorado Rockies. This was not to be a vacation for Jim, or a business trip. This junket to Colorado was to satisfy his curiosity over an artifact he had found while treasure hunting with his metal detector on an old abandoned farm in the nearby Illinois countryside. Jim's father had taught him all the tricks and techniques to treasure hunting with a metal detector, and the most important one had paid off his first time out since his father's passing. *"Always check around the fence posts first,"* his father had told him. *"Farmers often buried their valuables to protect them, and they would frequently use fence posts for reference points."*

Jim had remembered his father's advice when he had arrived at the abandoned farmhouse outside Rockaway, and the nearest fence line was where he had begun looking first. Twenty minutes into his treasure hunt he had received a strong signal. *I guess Pop was right,* he had thought, and had eagerly begun digging at the point where the signal had been the strongest. As he had scooped up the loosened earth with his hands he had felt something hard beneath his fingertips. Jim had then removed from the hole, a glass mason jar with a rusty, metal lid. As exciting as the find had been, when he had peered through the glass, all that had been inside was a folded piece of yellowed paper. He had hoped for a jar full of silver or gold coins, *but maybe, just maybe,* he had thought, *this paper might be valuable.*

Now, standing at his bedroom window watching the sunrise, he looked again at the yellowed piece of paper. It was a hand-drawn map, but, w*as this something some farm kid had contrived in some sort of game, or was it actually a map to something valuable and interesting?* Jim studied the map again, as he had a thousand times since finding it three months ago. There was nothing on the paper to indicate what it was a map to, other than the words, La Tanière Des Chats and Montagne De Père, and an X drawn high up on the side of what appeared to be a mountain in what appeared to be a small valley.

Excited over the possibilities, yet still uncertain of the map's authenticity, he had made the short drive to nearby Oleander in an effort to find someone at the university who could translate the words on the map. He had been directed to Professor Carlisle who had translated them for him, Tanière Des Chats meaning *Cats' Lair* and Montagne De Père translated to *Father Mountain*. It certainly sounded like a child's game, but he couldn't dismiss it based on that alone. It was just something that had gotten into his head that he couldn't let go of.

Encouraged by the fact that the words actually meant something and weren't just gibberish, he had stopped by the U.S. Geological Survey office where he had inquired about the name Father Mountain. Much to his surprise, and delight, he had been informed that there was actually a Father Mountain, located west-northwest of

Denver, Colorado near the Wyoming border. Jim ordered the most detailed map of the area that was available and it had been mailed to him the following week.

The hand-drawn Lair map had no orientation, no north or south marked on it, which made comparison to the topo map difficult, but the fact that Father Mountain did indeed exist had been enough to satisfy him that a trip out there was in order. *Why not? What else have I got to do? If someone took the time to draw a map to someplace, and then hide it away, there may be something very valuable there.* These were the thoughts that had set in motion Jim's quest for the Cats' Lair. *It may be a fool's folly,* he had thought, *but I'm going to do it!* The topo map he had purchased made no mention of a location called the Cats' Lair, but that made it all the more intriguing. He had then begun to think of the Cats' Lair as some secret place that only some old French explorer had known existed, and perhaps some long dead, Illinois farmer.

Jim's first concern had been to obtain time off from work. He had gone to his boss at Miller Foundry and had requested his vacation time at the first available opportunity. Mr. Miller found Jim's story very interesting, although in his opinion a bit of a lark, but Jim would now have two weeks to locate the Cats' Lair and solve the mystery of what it might be.

Having not been a camper in the past, Jim had visited the local sporting goods store in Oleander and had maxed out his Visa outfitting himself with everything he would need to live in the mountains for ten days. He fervently hoped that whatever he would find in the Cats' Lair would be valuable enough to pay off the Visa balance, because there was no way he could make the payments upon his return. As troubling as that thought was, it was something that would have to be worried over when he got home. Maxing out the Visa was the only way he could afford to purchase what he would need, so he had done it, prudence be damned.

Jim folded the map, placed it in his shirt pocket, and turned from the window. His Jeep was already loaded and ready to go, so there was only one thing left to do before leaving. Jim picked up the phone and dialed.

"Miller Foundry. How may I direct your call?"

"Hi Ruby. It's Jim. Put me through to 167, please."

"Sure, Jim. Have a great vacation!"

"Thanks, Ruby. I'll do that."

"Hello. That you Jim?"

"Yep, it's me, Red. Are you ready to go?" Jim asked.

"Absolutely! Let's hit the road! I've never been more ready for anything in my life! Get on over here!" Red exclaimed. "I just finished up the last of my inspections."

Red Porter had been Jim's best friend since before he could remember. They had gone to school together beginning in nursery school and continuing through high school. They had both graduated from Rockaway High three years ago, but neither had plans for college. Jim did remember a little about their friendship in kindergarten, but before that point in time he had only photos that his parents had taken to verify that they had been close ever since they were each two years old.

Jim had realized right away that he didn't really want to go into the Colorado wilderness alone and it would be much more fun if he had someone to share the adventure with. So, he had asked his best buddy and Red had jumped on the chance to go and hadn't stopped talking about it ever since. It took some serious talking to get their vacations at the same time, but, with a great deal of persistence, they had finally convinced Mr. Miller to see it their way. He had told them, "No way—before Independence Day", so they had had to wait until now.

Jim double-checked the front and back doors, and then went through the kitchen to the garage. *This is it,* he thought. Climbing into his Jeep, he pushed the button on the garage door remote, and then fired up the engine. *I sure hope this Cats' Lair turns out to be real,* he thought. *It would be a damn shame to come home with nothing to show for it but an old mason jar and a worthless map.* He backed out of the garage and headed for the foundry, thinking about the adventure, or misadventure, that lay ahead of them.

As he drove he thought about how he had wanted to get an earlier start this morning, but Red's shift at the foundry didn't end until seven a.m., when his vacation time would officially begin. It was now six forty-five and Jim would arrive at the foundry by seven, where he would pick up Red and they would head straight for Colorado.

They had already loaded all of Red's gear in the Jeep Saturday afternoon, so they could leave town directly from the foundry, Red sleeping a bit while Jim took the first shift driving. They planned to make the trip in two days, finding a campground to stay in their first night on the road and Jim had figured that would be somewhere in western Kansas or eastern Colorado.

So far, everything was going as planned and Red was waiting when Jim pulled into the parking lot.

"Hey, Red. Ready to shove off?" Jim asked.

"As ready as I'll ever be, amigo."

"Good, then the Cats' Lair awaits! Let's roll!"

Jim pulled the Jeep onto the highway and headed west. The adventure had begun and he was more than ready. He only hoped it would not all be in vain. He began reflecting on the map and why it may have been buried where it was. There had been no valuables in the jar, just the map. There had been no explanation on the map as to what the Cats' Lair might be. Jim thought how if the name had appeared on his topo map he would probably have dropped the whole notion of finding out about it. The fact of the Lair's omission from the topo map is what made it mysterious and intriguing. He had gone to the library in Oleander to see if he could find some reference to it, but there was no mention of it in any book on Colorado or the Rockies. Jim had even made a phone call to the sheriff's office in Clermont, Colorado, the closest town to where it should be, but the girl on the phone had no idea of what he was talking about, nor did the other person who was there with her. The Cats' Lair seemed to exist only on the one map that Jim had found beneath the base of an old fence post, and he hoped, somewhere on Father Mountain. Only time would tell.

❧   ❧   ❧

Jim and Red had decided not to use the Interstates to make the trip to Colorado, but rather the old highways. Although their destination of the Cats' Lair was the principal reason for their trip, this was their first time west of the Mississippi and they wanted to *actually* see the country between their home in Illinois and the Colorado Rockies. By six o'clock, as they pulled into a KOA campground, they had seen a lot and they were very impressed with the size and beauty of the country. They had made it all the way to Colorado the first day, but still had nearly the entire state to cross before reaching the Father Mountain area in the northwestern part of the state. Even though they had shared the driving, they were bushed and ready to settle in for the night.

The two friends built their first campfire and then sat and marveled at the stellar display overhead. It seemed not only brighter than at home, but also larger, by far, as well.

"Red—What do *you* make of the Cats' Lair?" Jim asked. "What do you think we are going to find out there on Father Mountain?"

"I have no idea, Jimbo. I suppose we may find a mountain lion or two, or perhaps a bobcat. The name had to come from something to do with cats. Beyond that, I haven't a clue."

"Why do you think there's no mention of it on any maps other than the one I found? Why does it appear that no one has ever even heard of it?"

Red looked at Jim with a curious expression and answered, "Why was it buried?" he asked. "That—is what puzzles me. That—and *who* buried it…"

"I tried to look into that and discovered that a man named Carter Elliott last owned the farm outright, but now the county has title due to back taxes owed on it by Carter Elliott. They've put it up for auction several times, but it hasn't been sold yet. I found that information in the public records. Beyond that, who knows who actually buried the jar," Jim replied. "Maybe Mr. Elliott himself, but that's just a guess. I wanted to get in touch with him and ask him if he knew about the map, but he's nowhere to be found. So, the big question is still, why was the map buried there in the first place?"

"True," Red commented, "But the biggest question is still—what is it?"

"And—that is what we'll find out in a couple of days—I hope!" replied Jim.

"When did this Carter Elliott give up the farm?" Red asked.

"He stopped paying the property taxes in 1930. The records state that he went west to look for ranch land and never returned. His family maintained the farm for years after that until the last of them died off in 1990. When the taxes went unpaid the county assumed title and it hit the auction block for the first time in 2000, just two years ago."

"Huh—Interesting. So the farm has been vacant for twelve years? Anybody could have buried that map during that time, or even before that."

"Yep. There's no way to know, but I think it was buried since the farm has been vacant. The jar is not an antique jar and the lid wasn't rusty enough to have been in the ground all that long."

"You know, Jim, the name Cats' Lair might be just a local name for something that is mentioned on your map," Red suggested.

"Yeah, I thought of that, too. The way the map's drawn though it is really hard to orient it correctly to the topographical map. The drawn map doesn't have any indication of what's up or what's down on it. I mean, no north or south. It's hard to know how to overlay it correctly, and the scales are different, of course. There are a bunch of names on the topo map for streams and valleys and such, but nothing I could find that has a thing to do with cats. If the Cats' Lair is a local name for something up there, it still doesn't appear to be known beyond that area."

"Well, that's what we are headed out there for. To *discover* it, right? Just like Hernando de Soto or Cabeza de Vaca. Ha! Now that's a name for an explorer—'Cow Head'! Maybe the Frenchman who found the Cats' Lair was named *Cat Head*," Red teased.

"Stow it, Red, and let's hit the hay. We still have a long drive ahead of us tomorrow."

Jim doused the fire and they slid into their sleeping bags for a night under the stars. It was, after all, a beautiful July evening and neither Jim nor Red had ever slept under the stars before. Neither of them had ever been much of the outdoors type, Jim having slept in a tent only once, and Red, never even that. This night under the Milky Way was quickly convincing them that their decision to take this trip had been a great one.

The drive across eastern Colorado was flat and tedious. Sure, the scenery was beautiful, with miles and miles of farm and rangeland to marvel at, but that was what Kansas had been all about, most of the day before. It was beginning to get old.

Clermont, Colorado was not much to speak of either, just a few run down businesses and several small homes. It was, however, the closest town to the jumping off point for Jim and Red's trek up to the Cats' Lair. Clermont was a sleepy little burgh at the east base of Father Mountain, and according to their maps, about twenty-two miles from the area in which they should find the Lair.

They had arrived just in time for supper at the Hummingbird Café, a small diner in the heart of Clermont's one street business district. Jim parked the Jeep in front of the little restaurant and they entered a world that seemed not to have changed since sometime in the 1950's. The Hummingbird was typical of what Jim and Red had both remembered seeing in movies about that era, and they were fascinated with it. Everything from the ceiling fans to the juke box in the corner was a delight to them.

"Damn, Red. Look at this place," Jim said, amazed at the sight.

"Yeah. This is awesome! I didn't know places like this still existed. Should we sit at the counter or in a booth?" Red asked Jim.

"Let's get a booth so we can try out one of those music things on the table. I've always wanted to use one of those ever since I saw them in that James Dean movie—ah—whatever it was called. You know the one I mean."

"I think so. Let's sit down and order. I'm famished," Red suggested.

Although the restaurant was small, and old, it was busy. Only two of the eight booths were open so they took the corner booth next to the jukebox. Only two or three minutes passed before the waitress came to their table and greeted them warmly, smiling a dazzling smile at them.

"Hi fellas. What's it going to be tonight? The special is roast beef and gravy with your choice of any two sides."

The boys stared at the beautiful waitress. Clermont was looking better already. She was about their age, perhaps twenty or twenty-one, and her hair was a striking blonde, long, straight, and shimmering with a healthy glow.

"Hi Laura," Jim replied, reading the waitress's nametag. *Boy, she's pretty*, he thought.

"Yeah, hi," answered Red, coming back to reality. "I'll try the special with a good hot cup of coffee, please. Mashed potatoes and creamed corn."

Red had finished his order, but continued to stare. He couldn't take his eyes off of her.

"Okay. Good choice. What'll you have," she asked, looking at Jim.

"I think I'll have the special also, but with a Coke, please," Jim answered. "I'll have the mashed potatoes, also, and green beans."

"Good. Two specials, a Coke and a coffee. You boys on vacation?" she asked, flashing a friendly smile their way.

"Well, sort of," replied Jim. "We came up to look for the Cats' Lair. Have you ever heard of it?" he asked, figuring now was as good a time as any to start their search. "By the way, I'm Jim, and this is Red," he said, pointing across the table to his buddy.

"Pleased to meet you both," she answered, smiling sweetly at Red. "The Cats' Lair? Sounds like a kids' game, doesn't it? What's it supposed to be, anyway, a motel or resort or something?"

"Well, to tell the truth, I'm not sure what it is supposed to be. For now it is just a name on an old map I found. I decided to take some vacation time and find out what it is, that's all," Jim told her, honestly.

"Well, good luck. I can't say that I have ever heard of it. Is it supposed to be near here?" she asked.

"About twenty miles from here, or thereabouts, up on Father Mountain," Jim informed her.

"Huh—Sorry, but I've lived here twenty years, all my life, and I've never heard mention of it. Good luck with your search. I'll get your supper out in a few minutes. By the way, where did you come from? Where's home?" she asked, turning back and smiling again at Red.

"Illinois," Red answered, beginning to blush.

"*That's* a drive!" she responded. "Supper will be out in a few."

Laura turned and headed back to the counter, flashing another smile in Red's direction as she went.

Strike one, Jim thought to himself. This was not a good start at all. If the Cats' Lair really existed, how could someone who had lived for twenty years within twenty miles of it, never have heard of it? *Not good*, Jim thought again.

"Let's try out this music box, Red," Jim suggested, dropping a nickel in the chrome plated music selector on the tabletop. "What do you want to hear?"

"To be perfectly honest with you, I don't recognize any of the songs," Red replied. "I don't think they've changed them since these machines were installed. What about that Laura though? I think she likes me. Did you see the way she smiled at me?"

"Yeah, I noticed that...Let's try A10. That looks good to me—*North to Alaska*—sort of reminds me of us, but for the fact that we came west—to Colorado."

Red laughed and added, "But I'll bet this Johnny Horton fella wasn't chasing some mythological place called the Cats' Lair!"

"No. You're probably right about that!"

With that, the two friends were silent, each taking in the ambiance of this quaint old restaurant and listening to Johnny Horton on the jukebox. Each was feeling that the trip was going to be a success, whether or not they found the Cats' Lair. They had seen a lot of beautiful country and they were each feeling more relaxed than they had remembered feeling in years. The Hummingbird Café was the icing on the cake. What a great little place.

"Excuse me," a voice said, from the next booth over. "Did I hear you boys mention the Cats' Lair?"

Jim turned and looked directly into the face of a very elderly man.

"I'm sorry. Harold Gillespie. Sorry to intrude," he added.

"No—that's okay, pleased to meet you. I'm Jim Preston, and this is my friend, Red Porter," Jim replied. "Yes. We mentioned the Cats' Lair. Have you heard of it?"

"Yes, but only once. I'd say it's a place to stay away from, if it exists."

"Why do you say that?" Jim asked, a little worried at Mr. Gillespie's comment.

"Well, I was just a boy, mind you, when I heard the name. I may never have remembered it at all if I hadn't seen with my own eyes what I saw. It was right here, in this diner, although it was called the Clermont Café back then, probably around 1930 or so. No, it *was* 1930. A fella, looked like a farmer to me, from Illinois or Indiana, forget which, came in asking questions about that place—your Cats' Lair place. Well, nobody had ever heard of it then, either, and the fella went off searching for it up on Father Mountain, or so he said he was going to do. He never came back."

"And—that's it?" asked Jim.

"No, that's not all," Mr. Gillespie, replied. Around 1990, I saw him again. Came right back into this diner, big as brass! Sixty years later! At first I didn't recognize him, but the more I stared at him the more familiar he became to me. I went over to the counter where he had seated himself and asked him if he had ever found the Cats' Lair he had gone looking for. That was the only way I could think of to verify that what I was seeing was for real and that it wasn't me that was going loony. Well, at first he looked totally dumbfounded, like I was crazy. Then, he tried to hide his recognizing the name by denying that he had ever heard of it, but I could tell, I was right on the money."

Mr. Gillespie just stared at Jim, like he was reliving the moment in his mind. He shuddered and slightly shook his head.

"So—he didn't want to reveal what he had found, you think—sir?" Jim asked.

"No, it was more than that. He didn't want to reveal that he was the same person that had come in here in 1930 asking about it. He didn't remember me, I was just a kid, and now I was seventy years old, so I was a total stranger to him. But, he knew I must have been in this diner that day back then. He put that much together, and he didn't want to acknowledge that it was him that was in here that day also."

"But—Why?" Jim asked, quite puzzled over the whole story.

"Because—he didn't look a day older than he did that day in 1930! That's why! How was he going to explain that? How was he going to explain remaining about thirty years old for sixty years time passed?"

"Naw. It must have been someone who looked like him. That's impossible," Red exclaimed before Jim had a chance to respond.

"Yeah. Red's right. It must have been someone else who just looked very similar to the guy you saw in 1930. After all, it *had* been sixty years since you first saw him," Jim replied.

"Nope. It was him, right down to the clothes he was wearing and the mole under his right eye. It was him," Mr. Gillespie insisted.

"Same clothes?" Jim asked.

"Yes sir, even the same clothes. Bib overalls, heavy, leather work boots, and a red plaid shirt. Even his sodbuster hat was the same. It was him all right, and that's why I say that the Cats' Lair would be a good place to stay away from!"

"If he ever found it," Red replied.

"Oh, he found it all right," Gillespie answered. "Whatever it is, it's the only explanation for what I saw here in 1990. The *only* explanation."

"But he denied any knowledge of it," Jim said.

"Wouldn't you? Anyway, that's the way I see it. You can draw your own conclusions and you can go up on Father Mountain if you want, but I hope for your sake you don't find that place you're looking for. That's all I have to say on the matter."

Harold Gillespie turned back into his booth and resumed his supper. Laura arrived shortly thereafter with Jim and Red's specials. Midway through their meal, Mr. Gillespie stood and began to leave, then turned and smiled at the boys. Then, turning slowly back, left the Hummingbird café. Red leaned forward and smiled at Jim, making a circling motion with his finger to his temple.

"That one's a loony bird for sure. '*He didn't look a day older than he did that day in 1930.*' Come on, where's he get that crap?" Red asked, snickering and grinning.

"I don't know, but it is a weird story. Too weird. Why would he make up something like that?" Jim asked.

"To string us along for kicks, that's why. He's a loony I'm telling you. What's he know? He just wanted to give a couple of strangers a hard way to go, that's all."

"Maybe, but that's a pretty wild story to come up with off the cuff, so to speak. Maybe we should find Gillespie and have another talk with him before we go traipsing off up that mountain. What do you think, Red?"

"Sure, if you say so. I can't wait to see what he comes up with next," Red joked. "Maybe he'll tell us that Father Mountain is inhabited by aliens from Pluto!"

"Okay, let's go," Jim said, laughing at Red's comments.

They stopped on the way to the cash register to ask Laura where they might find Harold Gillespie. They weren't prepared for her answer.

"Who?" she asked. "Do you mean the gentleman eating in the booth next to yours; the man you were talking with? I've never seen him before in my life. Why?" she asked.

"That's strange. He said that he's been in here before. We were talking about the Cats' Lair and he knew of it. We just wanted to ask him a few more questions about it before we head up that way," replied Red.

"Well, if he's been in here before, it has never been when I've been working. And—I can tell you one thing for sure, and that is that he doesn't live in Clermont, or anywhere else around here."

"Really? He just showed up for supper out of nowhere then? Red, this is…"

"Weird," Red said, finishing Jim's thought for him.

"Hey guys, we get people in here all the time that are passing through from Yellowstone to Rocky Mountain National Park. He may have been here before when I was off work. It wouldn't surprise me," Laura explained.

"Maybe, Laura. Maybe you're right. That's probably it, Red. He's just traveling through, got hungry and stopped for a bite to eat.—Say, Laura, is there a motel or campground anywhere around here?" Jim asked.

"Sure. There's a campground about a mile north of here. It's the Clermont KOA and it's right on the highway. You can't miss it. In fact you probably passed it on your way into town if you came by way of Denver," she answered.

"Thanks, Laura," Jim said. "If we have time we'll catch you at breakfast. Come on, Red. Let's get settled in for the night."

It was just like Laura had said and they had no trouble finding the campground. The Clermont KOA was quite a nice campground with flush toilets and hot showers, something both Red and Jim really appreciated after two long days on the road. After registering and locating their campsite, they took full advantage of the hot showers before retiring for the night. They decided to sleep under the stars again, but unfortunately, the evergreens at the camp were tall and thick. The wonderful smell of the pines, however, more than compensated for the lack of a stellar display. The two weary travelers drifted quickly off to sleep without further discussion of Gillespie or his fantastic tale.

CHAPTER 2

The Trip

The third day of their adventure began, literally, in the front seats of Jim's Jeep Wrangler. Choosing to sleep under the pine trees, Jim had not pitched the new tent he had purchased for their trip. Inexperience is a great teacher at the school of hard knocks and Jim and Red had just received their first lesson. It was at about two a.m. when the rains came and washed out their otherwise perfect night. Fortunately, the rain was light and they reacted quickly before their sleeping bags and clothing became too soaked. By sunrise, thanks to the extremely dry mountain air, they were pretty well dried out again.

Jim awoke before Red and stepping out of the Jeep, heard his boots crunch on the still moist soil. *This is cool*, he thought. *It's not muddy*. He reached down and scooped up a small handful of the soil and examined it. *Sort of gravely and sandy*, he thought to himself. He looked up through the pine boughs to a perfectly clear blue sky in all directions. *Looks like it's going to be a nice day.* He dropped the handful of soil and rubbed his hands together, briskly, rubbing them clean and walked around to the other side of the Jeep. Red was still fast asleep in the passenger seat, leaning against the door and snoring loudly. Jim took hold of the door handle, and preparing to catch Red, whipped the door open in one fast, sweeping motion.

"Hey! Damn!" Red cried out.

Jim caught Red halfway out the door and shoved him back up into his seat. Jim was a strong and powerful young man, the work at the foundry forming him into quite a muscular specimen. Still, it took all of his strength to shove Red back into his seat. Red's job at the foundry was what they called a *lazy man's* job and he was on the soft and portly side of the physical spectrum, a rather round two hundred and ten pounds, to be exact. He was not sloppy or blobby looking, merely rounded, as opposed to chiseled, and soft around the middle, giving one the impression that he moved about life as little as possible, relying on modern conveniences to do all of his work for him. The impression conveyed by his appearance was pretty much accurate.

"What the hell are you doing, shitbrick?" Red cried out.

"Morning, Red. Sleep well?" Jim asked.

"Yeah, just fine until you came along. What the hell did you do that for? I was dreaming about Laura."

"Oh yeah, what was your dream about?" Jim asked, still laughing.

"I don't know. It had just started when you yanked the door. She had just served us at the diner and then asked if she could go along with us to search for the Cats' Lair. She said she had some time off coming and it sounded like a cool adventure. *That's* when you yanked the door open!"

"Sorry."

"Like hell you are. I just wish you had let me finish my dream," Red replied, shaking his head and frowning at Jim.

"If you had finished it, you would never have remembered it," Jim reminded him.

"Yeah, maybe, but I doubt I would forget any dream about her. She's a fox, to say the least."

"Yeah, well forget about her. We're not taking her along with us, even if she would agree to go. We don't know what we're getting ourselves into, so we're not going to involve a sweet chick like her in the plan."

"Are you still worried about what Gillespie had to say?" Red asked Jim.

"Yeah, a little. I was thinking about it last night before I fell asleep and I hit on something I hadn't realized before," Jim announced. "Gillespie said that the guy looking for the Lair was a *farmer* from *Illinois!*"

"He said Illinois or Indiana, he couldn't remember which," Red interjected.

"Whatever. Either is close enough. How would he hit on those two states out of fifty states to choose from? I found the map on a farm in Illinois. Doesn't that seem rather a strange coincidence to you, Red?" Jim asked.

"Nope; not at all. You parked the Jeep right in front of the diner. He saw us arrive with Illinois license plates and used that information to validate his tale. There's no mystery to that," Red explained to Jim.

"Yeah, maybe, but I still think there is something to his tale, as far fetched as it may sound. You don't just make up something like that on the spur of the moment to give a couple of strangers a hard way to go. It just doesn't make any sense unless he truly believes his own story. Besides, what would be his motivation for telling us something like that if it weren't true? What's he got to gain?"

"Jim—Some people are just like that. It's that simple. Strangers are who you screw with when they come into your town. It's as simple as that," Red said.

"But…Clermont isn't his town. Laura said she has never seen him before and that he doesn't live there. What about that?"

"So—maybe for some reason he doesn't want us snooping around up there?"

That's more along the lines of what I was thinking," Jim stated. "But why?"

"I don't know, so let's say he was on the level. So what? There is still absolutely no plausible explanation for what Gillespie believes he saw. So why worry yourself about it? Let's just go find the place, if we can, and see for ourselves," Red answered.

"Yeah—I guess you're right. Should we go to the diner and get some breakfast before we leave? I know I'm hungry."

"Now that sounds good to me," Red answered. "Maybe Laura will be working this morning and I can drool over her again," he laughed.

"You worry me, Red. You're thinking far too much about Laura and you're going to get hurt. Look at her. You know she has to have a boyfriend," Jim cautioned his friend.

"I know. It's just the way she smiled at me—twice. Maybe I'm reading more into it than I should, but she did seem to like me, didn't she?"

"I don't know, Red. Girls like her don't look at guys like us. You know that."

Not in Illinois, they don't, Red thought. *But maybe in Colorado—they do...*"Yeah, right," he answered.

Before leaving for breakfast, they laid their sleeping bags out over their gear in the back of the Jeep so they could finish drying out and then headed for the Hummingbird Café. Laura was on duty and Red did drool over her, again, but not overtly. He managed to keep his enthusiasm for Laura under control, but barely. Breakfast was good and quite welcomed by the boys, the bacon having been fried just right and the eggs, delicious, and the homemade blueberry waffles had been divine. They finished their meal, rubbing their swollen stomachs and feeling a little sleepy from the quantity of food they had consumed. Laura brought their check to the table, smiling, as it seemed she did constantly.

"How was breakfast, Red?" she asked. "Jim?"

"It was great, and way too much food," Red was quick to reply.

"You look like you can handle it, Red," she answered, smiling.

"Oh yes. No problem there," he said, firing back his sweetest smile at her.

"So, are you guys leaving for that Lair place you came to find?"

"Yep, just as soon as we digest a little of that breakfast," Jim answered.

"You know, I've got some time off coming. Would you fellas mind if I tagged along? I'm pretty good in the forest and I've done a lot of hiking on Father Mountain. I know where to find water and all."

Jim just stared at Red, who shrugged his shoulders in disbelief. Jim was beginning to get the feeling that there was something very strange going on around here. First the fantastic tale the mysterious Gillespie had told, and now, Red's dream materializing right before their eyes.

"Laura, why would you ask to come along?" Jim asked her, in an openly suspicious tone.

"I don't know—I had a dream about it last night; just the three of us up there on the mountain, camping and all. It sounds like fun, and you guys seem like nice guys, that's all. To tell the truth, I *am* kinda bored with this life of mine, waiting tables all day and going home each night to an empty house. It just sounds like a good change of pace for me. Something interesting to do for a change."

"Jim—Why fight it? It's in the cards," Red said. "Besides, we could use someone who knows her way around up there," he finished.

"I don't know, Red. After what Gillespie had to say, I'm not sure I want to involve someone else in this thing. Laura, did you hear what Gillespie had to say; his *warning*, so to speak?" Jim asked her.

"No. I didn't hear what he had to say. Why?" she asked.

"Well, he had a pretty far fetched story to tell related to the Lair, or so he seemed to believe. Something about a guy he saw here in this café in 1930 and then again in 1990. He said the man hadn't aged a day in sixty years! He told us that the first time he saw the man he was asking about the Lair. Pretty weird stuff, if you ask me," Jim told her.

"Cool. That sounds like a real adventure! There is a story though, like that," Laura told them.

"Really?" Jim asked. "What sort of a story?"

Laura thought for a minute, and then replied, "Well, it's about an Indian that wandered into town from Father Mountain one day and freaked out right in the middle of Main Street! The sheriff had to arrest him for being a public nuisance because he sat down in the middle of the street and started chanting something about Chief Cleveland and broken promises. Nobody could figure out what he was talking about and he wouldn't get up and move out of the street, so Sheriff Cramer took him to jail."

"When was this?" Red asked.

"About four years ago, around '98, I guess," Laura answered.

"What happened to him?" Jim asked, fascinated with the story.

"The sheriff called in an interpreter because the Indian's English was poor and the interpreter talked with him for a while, getting his story. It seems that the Indian claimed that only six 'moons' before, President Cleveland had promised his people the land Clermont was built on. Now, he said, just six months later we had built a village and a stone road right on their promised lands. Crazy—huh…?"

"What ever happened to him?" Red asked.

"He disappeared. The sheriff decided to keep him for the night and try to find someone to claim him the next morning. When he went in to check on him in the morning, he was gone. The cell door was open and he was long gone. Sheriff Cramer figured someone snuck in the jail overnight and let him out. It was the only explanation he could think of."

"Too weird," Jim replied.

"Way too weird," Red confirmed.

"I'll say," Laura commented. "He was about eighteen years old, yet he claimed that President Cleveland had made that promise only six months prior to this!"

"See!" Jim said. "Laura, are you sure you want any part of this? First there's Gillespie's weird story, then Red dreams that you want to come along with us, and finally, there is the Indian story! And—it all seems to be tied to the Cats' Lair, somehow."

"Wait. How do you figure that?" Red asked. "Only Gillespie's story is directly linked to that place, and that's loose, if you ask me. The dream is just a coincidence and the Indian came down from Father Mountain, true enough, but no one said anything about the Cats' Lair, did they, Laura? You said you never heard of it before, right?"

"Right. No one said anything about such a place in regard to the Indian's story," she replied.

"See, Jimbo. There's no evidence to bear out your worries about the Lair. Let's just get up there and try to find it. We can deal with what we find, *when* we find it—if we do," suggested Red.

"Okay then, what about Laura? Do we take her along? Laura—when could you leave if we decide to include you on this expedition?" Jim asked her.

"Tomorrow morning. I'll get my friend Alice to fill in for me here at the diner. She's always willing to earn a little extra since she retired from here last year. Would that be soon enough?"

"What do you say, Jim? Yes or no?" Red asked.

"I say okay. Let's do it! You and I can go see how far the roads will take us and how far a field my Jeep will take us tomorrow when we actually go looking. It'll give us one less day to search for the Lair, but it won't be a total waste of a day."

"Okay then, it's decided. Laura, you get hold of Alice and make your arrangements and Jim and I will go see how much of a hike we'll have to get up to the Lair's location. We'll take the Jeep as far as is possible, but there is going to be some serious hiking involved in this. We'll find out today just how much and get a feel for the mountain."

"You won't get your Jeep any distance off the end of 27," Laura advised them. "The trees are too densely packed up there. There's no room for your Jeep to maneuver between them. There is an old logging road off of 27 that would take you further in, but I doubt if you'd ever find it. It doesn't look like a road anymore and you pretty much have to know where it is or you'll miss it every time, but go anyway and start getting your bearings if you want. Have a look around and if you find that old road, I'll buy your breakfast."

"Deal!" Red exclaimed.

"What's 27?" Jim asked her.

"Access Road 27. It's the only road up into the Father Mountain area," she informed him. "If you are going up Father, that's the only way in."

Laura cleared away their breakfast dishes and Jim spread his topo map out on the table. He followed Access Road 27 with his finger to its terminus. He tapped his finger on the spot on the map.

"This is as far as we go in the Jeep according to Laura. Okay, so where do we go from there? I think up and to the west judging from the Lair map."

After a few more minutes of study, Jim folded the map and the boys paid their bill at the Hummingbird, moving their discussion to the Jeep. They studied the topo map again, checking for any four-wheel drive roads that might lead off of the access road. After several minutes careful study, they determined that Laura had been correct. There were none.

Jim had no problem with hiking a bit, but Red was already having a problem with the altitude at seven thousand feet in Clermont. Comparing the old map Jim had found to the topo map, it appeared that the Lair rested in a small valley at approximately eleven thousand feet. This not only concerned Jim, but also brought up serious questions as to Red's ability to hike at those elevations. Jim was a jogger and in pretty good physical shape, but Red, on the other hand, was a bit of a couch potato. Actually, he was nearly totally sedentary. Even his job at the foundry did not require much movement on Red's part. Red's job at the plant was all a matter of paperwork and no physical activity, while Jim, quite to the contrary, lifted heavy steel all day long. Jim could easily see that Red might have a problem up there. As far as Laura was concerned, she would probably run circles around them both. Jim wasn't worried about her at all, considering Laura looked as fit as she did fancy and was acclimated to this country.

"If there are any four-wheel drive roads up there, Red, they're not on this map. This Access Road 27 gets us in as close as we are going on graded road. We'll just have to take it from there the best we can. Maybe we'll find a four-wheeler road once we get up there, but from what Laura said, that's doubtful."

"Don't worry about me, Jim. I'll be fine. Let's just get going," Red replied.

"Who said I was worrying about you, you buffoon?" Jim asked.

"I can tell what you're thinking. You think this is going to be too rough on a couch potato like me. Right? Sure it is, I can see it in your face and hear it in your voice. '*Why did I ever bring the doughboy along?*' is exactly what you are asking yourself right about now, isn't it? Fess up!"

"Gee, Red. Where did all that hostility come from? Yes, I'm concerned for your well-being, but I don't regret bringing you along at all. If there is something worth sharing up there in the Cats' Lair, you are the one person that I want most to share it with. We're buddies, and always will be, so calm down a little, please."

"Well, you seem awfully intent on getting in as close as possible. I just thought…"

"Well think again, Red," Jim interrupted. "I want to get in close for my own benefit as well as yours. Neither one of us is acclimated to those altitudes up there. It would be rough on *anyone* from the

Midwest flatlands. Let's just head up there and see what we find. Ready?"

"Ready, and—sorry I snapped at you," Red apologized.

Jim pulled the Jeep onto Main Street and drove out of town in the direction of Access Road 27, which they found easily, seven miles down the road. Thirty-five minutes later they were at the end of the graded access road, sitting at an elevation of about ten thousand feet in total awe of the size and beauty of the forest. They had truly never been anyplace like this in their lives and realized that the photos they had seen in books did not begin to do justice to country like this.

"This appears to be the end of the line, Red. Let's have a look at the map and see where we are," Jim suggested.

Red pulled the map from the glove compartment and they studied it intently. They located the end of the access road and determined that there would be about a two-mile hike to the Lair's valley and all uphill another thousand feet.

"That's going to be some climb," Red said, already exhausted at the thought.

"Don't let the sound of the thousand feet scare you, Red. It's not that much elevation over two miles of ground. It's uphill to be sure, but not *that* steep. And—remember, we'll probably have to walk four miles to cover the two miles on the map. I'm sure there is no way in hell we can walk straight to it. We'll be fine, you'll see. It just *sounds* like a difficult climb when you're thinking ahead to it."

Jim hoped he had allayed some of Red's concerns. It really didn't appear to be such a bad hike, and that was what concerned him. If the hike was as routine as it appeared on the map, why then, was the Cats' Lair unknown to everyone, apparently, other than Gillespie, the farmer from Illinois or Indiana, and whoever drew the map he had found? So far, no one else, including the U.S. Geological Survey seemed to have any idea that such a place, whatever it is, exists. Perhaps the Indian that wandered down off of Father Mountain knew, but there was no proof of that.

But, everyplace has a name, Jim thought. *Some places have even more than one name. Some places have an official name and a popular local name, but there is no place that has yet to be discovered, not any more.*

"You know, Red. Something is not adding up here," Jim said, climbing out of the Jeep. "Hand me the topo map and the Lair map. I want to compare them again."

"Sure, what are you looking for?" Red asked.

"I'm not sure, but I think I must have overlooked something. The Cats' Lair has to have a name, even if it's something different than the Cats' Lair. Nothing is *unnamed* anymore."

Jim spread the topo map out on the hood of the Jeep and placed the hand drawn Lair map over it. Although the hand drawn map did appear to be drawn roughly to scale, the two maps were not drawn to the same scale so there was no way they would fit neatly over one another. It was a matter of identifying the same points on each map and then superimposing the drawn map onto the topo map.

"Red, there's a small marker in the glove box. I want to double check some things here."

"Sure," Red replied, and fetched the marker for Jim. "What's the problem? I thought you had this all figured out already."

"So did I, but I think I've missed something. I know there's no Cats' Lair marked on this map, but there should be *some* name for the place. If we knew the accepted name, or local name for the place, people might know what we are talking about and shed some light on it for us."

"Who cares? We'll find out all we need to know when we get up there, right? I mean, why bother with the locals around here?" Red asked.

"I was thinking of Laura. If we could put a name to this place that she would recognize, she could probably take us straight to it. She said she has hiked all over Father Mountain. It could save a lot of time and energy if we knew exactly where we were going before we left."

Jim began with the first prominent marking on the Lair map, a switchback bend in a stream that cut horizontally across the map. He located such a spot on the topo map, and circled it. He then picked the crest of Father Mountain as the second point, which he again circled on the topo map. He oriented the Lair map to these two points on the topo map and projected where the X would fall on the topo map. If he was reasoning correctly the Lair should be on the west face of Father Mountain, high up in a small valley. Jim was pretty sure he had it figured correctly, but the valley didn't appear to have a name. He looked more closely. This area of the map was cluttered with elevation lines all converging on one another at this point, indicating some pretty steep terrain. It also made it very hard to discern any names that may be hidden among the jumble of elevation lines, water features and what have you. He studied the valley intently, turning the map to different angles, until he saw the letter "V". It was the only discernable letter and it was very small.

"Look, Red! The letter "V"! This valley does have a name! I can't make it out with all the clutter in this area of the map. What I need is a frickin' magnifying glass. Let's head back to town and see if we can find a place to buy one."

"Let me take a look," Red replied.

Red leaned over the map and studied the area Jim had indicated to him.

"What you need—is a pair of glasses, Jimbo. It says, '*Lynx Canyon*'. There's no frickin' "V" in there! Man, talk about the blind leading the blind. When was the last time you had your eyes checked?" Red asked, laughing.

"Shit," Jim answered. "I didn't realize I was that bad off. Lynx Canyon, huh—Let me see that again—Naw, I still don't see it. Are you sure?" Jim asked.

"Yeah, I'm sure. It's as plain as day. Lynx Canyon—Right there in black and white—Lynx Canyon, with no 'V,'" Red confirmed, smiling devilishly at Jim.

"Cool! That has something to do with cats for sure! Let's get back to town and see if that rings a bell with Laura. Maybe she knows the place. Hell, maybe she has been there before. Come on, get in the Jeep and we'll go find out."

They scrambled back into the Jeep and headed back to Clermont, encouraged by their new discovery. Perhaps Laura would know something of Lynx Canyon, perhaps not, but it was something more than they knew a few moments ago.

On the drive back to town, Jim began thinking about the new name they had for the valley indicated by the X on the Lair map. Lynx Canyon. That certainly indicated the presence of cats, much like the name Cats' Lair. Perhaps they were one in the same. He certainly hoped so, but now that the valley had a name, which seemed official, it meant that it was a known place. He suspected as much from the start, but he had hoped he was looking for something not commonly known. Then it hit him. He had touched on it briefly before, but it hadn't registered. Perhaps the Cats' Lair was something *located in* Lynx Canyon, not the valley itself. Perhaps the valley was generally known, but not the Lair.

Jim pulled the Jeep into the closest parking space to the Hummingbird's front door and jumped from the Jeep almost before it had stopped rolling. He flung open the door to the café and stood, looking around for Laura. He spotted her back at the last booth by the jukebox and rushed to her.

"Lynx Canyon. Ever hear of that?" he asked, in a breathy whisper.

Laura was in the middle of taking an order and held up her finger indicating that Jim should wait a minute. She continued taking the order while Jim waited anxiously.

"Thanks, folks. I'll have your meal out to you shortly."

Turning to Jim, "Now what's this about Lynx Canyon?" she asked.

"Have you ever heard of it?" Jim asked, again.

"Sure, it's lovely up there. Why?"

"Then you've been there?"

"Yes, Jim, twice. What's this all about, anyway?" Laura questioned.

"I think that the Cats' Lair is somewhere in Lynx Canyon," Jim explained.

"Well, if it is, I've never seen it. Of course, it would help to know what the heck the Cats' Lair is supposed to be. Honestly, Jim, I don't think what your looking for is in that valley. I've spent the better part of five days camped in that valley and I never saw anything you might call the Cats' Lair. Is it some sort of landmark or formation or something like that?"

"I don't know, Laura. I can't tell you anything more than that according to my map it should be in that valley, whatever it is. That's all—Let me ask you this. While you were up there did you ever see any cats? Mountain lions or bobcats or the like?" Jim asked.

"Well, yes. I saw bobcats, quite a few. They seem to favor that valley for some reason. It's probably the remoteness and denseness of it. It's good shelter for them I imagine."

"Yes! See, Laura, I'm assuming the name Lynx Canyon comes from the fact that a lot of bobcats frequent the valley, but I would think the name Cats' Lair suggests that there are a lot of them born and living up there. Perhaps there is a specific part of the canyon where they breed and bear their young. Have you ever seen a place like that up there?"

"No, Jim, I can't say that I have, but then again, I wasn't looking for anything like that while there. I was just camping and enjoying the solitude," she explained.

"That's okay. At least you can take us directly there. That's better than I could hope for before. That will save a lot of time and trouble for us. You *are* still interested in going, aren't you?"

"Sure, tomorrow morning, early. I've already arranged for Alice to take my shifts for a week. I'm ready to go," she said, enthusiastically.

"Great! Where do we pick you up?" Jim asked.

"At my place, the last house on the left as you're leaving town to the south. It's a yellow brick ranch. You'll see it plain enough."

"What time will you be ready to go? I was thinking about six o'clock, if that's okay?"

"Six is fine, Jim. I'll see you then. Ah—Where's Red?"

"He's waiting in the Jeep, 'conserving energy', or so he says."

"Well, tell him I said hello, okay?"

"Yeah—sure, will do."

Jim went back out to the Jeep where Red had dozed off. He was conserving energy all right. Jim broke the good news to him about Laura knowing where to find Lynx Canyon and even having been there. Red just smiled a weak smile.

"What's wrong, Red. You're not getting cold feet are you? You're still up for this, right?"

"Yeah, sure, Jim. I'm okay. It's just that if Laura already knows about Lynx Canyon, what's the whole point? I mean the mystery is gone. It's there; she's been there, end of story. Nothing."

"No, not at all. She's still never heard of the Cats' Lair or seen anything up there that it might be. *That's* the mystery! It's not the canyon itself. It's the Lair," Jim explained, trying to be as up beat as he could be. "Really, Red—It's going to be cool—you'll see! And—ah—by the way, Laura says 'Hello.'"

Red came immediately full awake.

"Really?" he asked.

CHAPTER 3

The Observers

"**Y**our move, Malic."

"Oh, sorry, Damon. I was thinking about the boys," Malic apologized. "I fear they did not take my story of Carter Elliott seriously."

"Yes, I fear you are right, and furthermore, when Laura told them of Little Hawk, again they were not deterred."

"Our best laid plans, Damon?" Malic commented.

"Yes, Malic. Our best laid plans seem not to discourage these young men," Damon admitted.

"But, still, your idea to involve Laura for her story of Little Hawk was a stroke of genius," Malic said, complementing his mentor. "But, I've been wondering about something. How did Little Hawk escape the jail? You never told me the end of the story."

Damon smiled and winked.

"Damon—You let him out!" Malic exclaimed. "Whatever became of him?"

"I took him far into the forest and told him that the Great Spirit did not want him back in that area again, which, was the truth. The Father didn't want him telling too many more people about his experience."

"Good move, Damon. Still in all, your plan to have Laura convey the story to the boys was a good one."

"It would have been had her story succeeded in dissuading them from continuing their quest. Now, however, I fear that all my cleverness has simply added another of the Kinder to the mix," Damon confessed.

"It might have worked, Damon. Don't be so critical of yourself in this matter. I am sure you'll think of something before it's too late. My move...Bc4."

"Ah—I see your own cleverness is improving...Qh5. Have you been to the window lately?" Damon asked.

"No, not in a while," Malic answered.

"Then perhaps we should go now. I feel a strange need to pay close attention to those two. I believe that if they gain access their youth will drive them further than Carter Elliott's efforts took him. We had better go see what they are up to at this point in time."

Damon pushed back his chair from the table and proceeded from the chamber, followed closely by Malic. They turned right, going down the perfectly cylindrical passage formed through the smooth gray stone. Their passage was silent, not even their footsteps being audible. Another right turn brought them face to face with Otheon.

"Otheon, good day to you," Damon greeted. "What brings you down into this passage?"

"I have just come from your window, in search of you, Damon. Perhaps you can explain what I have just seen."

"Perhaps, Otheon. What is it that concerns you?" Damon asked.

"The two boys. I have just seen them in their campground and heard them discussing Lynx Canyon. *That* is what concerns me! Their conversation sounded for all the world as if they are still planning a search for the portal. I was under the impression that you were taking care of the matter, Damon."

"Yes, Otheon. Malic and I are working on a solution now. Our first attempts at discouraging them have failed, but we are not through trying by any means. We fully understand the importance of our success in this matter."

"Unfortunately, Damon, you may not use *any means.* As important as this is, please remember that you may only use mistruths, deception, and trickery to achieve your goal. So it is written and must be obeyed."

"Yes, Otheon, we understand the Father's wishes," Damon replied.

"Good. Carry on, Damon."

Otheon walked on, leaving Damon and Malic to consider his words.

"What now?" asked Malic.

"We proceed to the window and watch and listen. Perhaps the boys will give us a clue as to what our next move should be."

Damon and his aide proceeded down the smooth gray corridor, until they came to the Falls of Knowledge, a waterfall within Father Mountain, which separated the rest of Ahveen from Damon's windowed chamber. Damon passed through the falls first and Malic closed his eyes, and then followed.

"When will I ever learn?" Malic asked, facing Damon, dripping wet.

Damon, who was completely dry, smiled and said, "When you do, Malic. When you do. Then and only then will you emerge from the falls as you entered. The answer is within you. Reach inside and find it there. It is all a part of becoming a Guardian. When you have full control of your environment, then and only then can you hope to control others'. Reach within yourself and eventually you will find the answer, my friend."

"But why must this lesson be so—so wet?" Malic complained, frowning at his inability to remain dry as Damon could do.

"It is simply motivation. When you become tired of getting wet, you'll find the answer."

"I *am* tired of getting wet, yet I still do. There must be more."

"There is no more, Malic. All the answers you need are within you. They will come," Damon assured him. "They will come."

"May I dry myself now?" Malic asked.

"Certainly, go ahead, but be quick. I wish to check on the boys."

Malic became the bobcat and shook himself profusely, sending droplets of water from his fur glistening down the corridor walls. As quickly as he had become the bobcat, he returned to his own form.

"Feel better?" Damon asked.

"Much," replied Malic, happy to be dry once again.

The Guardian and his aide entered the windowed chamber and looked out into the forest. There was no visible separation between the chamber and the outside world. One entire wall of the chamber *was* the forest. The appearance was as if one could take one step forward and *be* in the forest outside. This was, however, an illusion. This was merely the window from which Damon and Malic kept watch over the Kinder. Each Guardian had his own window, focused on the period of time for which he was responsible. It had been this way from the day of creation and would remain this way until the last Kinder breathed his last breath on Earth.

Although the window was a mere illusion, a tool for seeing all at all times, the portal was not an illusion. The portal was the functional means by which the Guardians could enter the world at whatever time in the world's history they chose to do so. Normally, this choice was made by the needs of the Kinder. In the case of the two boys, Red and Jim, the need lately had been to preserve the one-way flow of time.

Both Damon and Malic knew that this emergency had occurred before, once with Little Hawk and then again, with Carter Elliott. In each of those crises Damon's efforts had proved enough to preserve the proper flow, but the boys had him worried. His biggest fear was the obstinacy of youth. Little Hawk had been young, but superstitious. He did not believe that these twenty-first century boys would have the same fears of the unknown.

Damon focused on the window and the image of the forest blurred, then almost instantly cleared to reveal Red and Jim sitting by their campfire at the KOA campground. Damon listened as the boys discussed their plans for the morning. It became quite clear within minutes that he and Malic had failed thus far to dissuade the boys from their chosen course.

"Malic, my trusted friend, I fear we must try harder. They are not the least bit occupied with fears of the unknown. They scoff at the stories of Little Hawk and Carter Elliott."

"That, Damon, is because they do not yet believe the stories. As you said, they are of the twenty-first century. Superstition does not run their lives. They are from an analytical world of science and *proven* laws of physics. If they locate the portal and have the courage to enter it, then—when they emerge, they will begin to understand that not all is explained through their science."

Damon stared at Malic. A broad smile slowly formed upon his face.

"Well Blessed Father! My dear Malic, I do believe you are well on your way to graduation. Your observation is worthy of the highest order of Guardians. But, it still behooves us to try to prevent their entry. It is the safest way. Come—Let us finish our game."

Damon turned and passed through the Falls of Knowledge. Malic followed and emerged dry. Damon smiled and turned toward his chambers and the conclusion of their game, while Malic stood motionless, marveling at his dry clothes, and then rushed quickly to catch up with Damon.

"Congratulations," Damon said, as Malic rejoined him.

"Thank you, Damon, but I still do not know how I did it," Malic confessed.

"I never said you would ever understand it or be conscious of how you achieved it. I merely stated that what you needed to know would come from within you. It is accomplished by attaining a higher level of understanding of how all things that are, fit together with one another. I believe your arriving at your understanding of the twenty-first century boys more than likely raised your overall awareness to the required level. Again, congratulations, dear Malic."

"Thank you, Damon. It feels good to reach this level, and—dry. But, Damon, I do have one question to ask about something I do not understand. Why is it that we never see another Guardian or aide at the window?" Malic asked.

"Because that is my window, assigned to me by Otheon. There are many others, each assigned to a different Guardian, each in turn assigned to a different time period of the world, beginning at creation and continuing throughout eternity. It is very complex, Malic. Don't ask me to explain it. Don't even ask Otheon. Only the Father understands what He created when it comes to this. We merely utilize the gift in the spirit it was intended, to help worthy Kinder in time of peril. We understand how to do this, but we do not understand how it all comes together by the time our efforts reach what is known as the present. Only the Father knows this. We are merely the emissaries of His good will."

"Have you ever met with the Father?" Malic asked.

"I have not. Archangels carry out all communications between Heaven and Ahveen. But, when I am retired to Heaven I trust I will get the opportunity to meet Him. It is something I look forward to very much."

"And I."

Damon stopped and cocked his head as if listening to something in the distance.

"Ah—It is time for meeting. We will have to finish our chess game later, Malic."

"Exactly what is it you hear at this time each day, Damon," Malic asked. "I heard nothing."

"You will. It is the call to the meeting of Guardians. Otheon issues it at this time each day. One day you will hear it, too. Be patient, Malic. It will not be much longer."

Upon entering the hall through the main entry, Malic was over-whelmed as usual. In the relatively short period of time he had been in Ahveen he had not yet grown accustomed to the sight. The hall itself was massive. He envisioned it as occupying the entire center of Father Mountain, but of that he could not be certain. Never the less, it was immense and not unlike a gargantuan cathedral. The ceiling was vaulted of smooth gray stone rising hundreds of feet above his head. On the floor of the hall were rows upon rows of gracefully curving pews stretching for hundreds of feet in either direction forming concentric semi-circles to the sidewalls. There was one large central aisle, which ran from the main entry to the alter, and at least fifty lesser aisles radiating out from the alter like spokes on a wheel. It was an impressive site, but as thousands of Guardians filled the hall the spectacle became overpowering and breathtaking.

The majority of the meeting itself was not unlike any church ser-vice Malic remembered from his years as a Kinder in his homeland of Olin. There were prayers offered, hymns were sung, and Otheon spoke from the pulpit the words of the Father as brought down to him by the archangels. More hymns followed and the meeting always concluded with an update on what was occurring on the outside among the Kinder. This was done for the benefit of the majority of Guardians who were responsible for time rings of the Earth's *past*. This was of great importance to these Guardians as it helped them understand the results of their efforts in their rings.

The actual nature of time within Father Mountain was simply that there was no past, present, or future. All time was concurrent within Ahveen. This was known as the Complexity, which only the Father understood. It wasn't that a particular Guardian, assigned to a time ring in the Middle Ages, was working in the past. It was simply that his vision was limited to that period. In an effort to help him under-stand what his deeds performed then, on the outside, meant to the world outside in the present, he needed to understand the state of the world outside which was beyond his vision. The Complexity, then, was the knowledge of how it all melded into a streamlined and even, forward flow of time on Earth.

Following the meeting, Damon and Malic returned to Damon's chambers and concluded their chess game. Damon, as usual, was the victor. Malic then did something that he had never done in the past. He offered to return to the window and check on the boys.

"Thank you, Malic. I'll remain here and work on my journals," Damon said, surprised at the offer. "Do you mind if I ask why you have made this offer for the first time ever?"

"No, not at all. It will be the first time I will remain dry upon entering and leaving the windowed chamber," Malic advised Damon, laughing.

"Oh—I see," Damon said, smiling. "Then by all means, go and enjoy your new talent."

Malic left Damon and traveled the corridor to the windowed chamber, passing through the Falls of Knowledge and emerging dry within the windowed chamber. He smiled. In his former life he never minded getting wet. He remembered swimming and bathing and wave riding in particular, so he never quite understood why he despised it so much here in Ahveen. The only explanation for his aversion to water was that it must have something to do with his acquired ability to become the bobcat. He seemed to remember, once again from his life among the Kinder, that cats had an aversion to getting wet. Perhaps it was true of bobcats also.

He looked at the window and out to the forest. Concentrating, as Damon had taught him, he focused his thoughts on the boys. The image in the window blurred and then became sharp once again. Their fire had died down, but he could see Red and Jim sleeping peacefully by the fire's dim glow. Malic smiled at the boys and prayed for their salvation.

CHAPTER 4

The Climb

*T*uesday morning was crisp and clear, the temperature mild, and the skies cloudless. It looked like the perfect day to begin their quest for the Lair. Jim was the first to awake and looked quickly at his watch. *Good,* he thought. *We still have half an hour to get to Laura's.*

"Hey, Red. Wake up," Jim ordered, shaking Red's arm. "We've got to get a move on. Laura will be wondering where we are if we don't shove off soon."

"Okay, okay—quit shaking me. I'm up! What's the rush?" Red asked, through a huge yawn.

"What's up is that it's five thirty and we told Laura six o'clock. We've gotta move. Besides, today's the day we get our first look at Lynx Canyon. Let's shake it!"

They crawled out of the sleeping bags, rolled them up and placed them in the back of the Jeep. Jim checked the fire to make sure it was out and they hit the road.

Jim was bright and cheerful, Red, still very groggy and grumpy. Red was definitely not the morning person, and it showed. They headed back toward town and soon came to Laura's house, which sat back from the road about one hundred feet. Jim pulled the Wrangler into the gravely drive and beeped the horn as he drew near the house. Laura was out the door immediately and walked to the garage door, bending down to raise it.

"Where are you going, Laura?" Jim yelled to her.

"I'm getting my gear. I have it all laid out here in the garage," she yelled back to him.

Jim had not thought of that before. He turned and looked into the back of his Jeep. There was very little room left, even with the back seat folded forward.

"You're going to love this, Red," Jim said to his buddy, smiling.

"Love what?"

"Laura is going to have to sit on your lap until we get up to the end of the access road. That's what!" Jim replied.

"Yeah! Cool! I knew something good would come of this trip!"

Red still had designs on Laura, which had begun just as soon as he had first seen her. She was beautiful, that was obvious to anyone with half an eye for beauty. But the bigger attraction was her friendliness and sweetness, which radiated from her like light from the Sun. Laura had a fervent desire to do more than spend the day waiting tables and the evenings, sitting home alone. What made her jump on the opportunity to go along on the adventure was much the same as what made Jim and Red come out here in the first place. There had to be more than the work-a-day world, which had been their daily existence up until this time.

"Well, I better go break the news to her before she gets over here and discovers it on her own," Jim said.

"Yeah, maybe you had better," agreed Red.

Jim went over to the garage where Laura was picking up the last of her gear.

"Hey, Laura. We have a bit of a problem."

"What's that, Jim?" she asked, looking up and smiling.

"Well—I didn't think this too far ahead and it seems that with all our gear in the back of the Jeep, the only place for you is on Red's lap," he informed her, nervous over what her reaction might be.

"Oh—Well—Hey, why not take my Cherokee? I think we would all be more comfortable in it, and it can go almost anywhere your Wrangler can. Not only that, but that way Red won't be too embarrassed," Laura answered, winking at Jim and smiling her gorgeous smile.

"Sounds like a great idea, if you don't mind. I'm sure Red will be relieved," Jim said, returning the wink.

"Hey, Red! Start bringing our stuff over here!" Jim yelled back to the Jeep.

Red looked a bit confused, but climbed out of the Jeep and began hauling their gear over. Jim went back to help him move it to the Cherokee and explained the plan to him as they worked. Red wasn't sure what had transpired in the garage to bring about this move, but he was secretly glad it had taken place. He was fond of Laura, but he was also on the shy side when it came to girls and ever since Jim had mentioned her riding in his lap, he had been quite nervous about it. He was just that way.

They had Laura's vehicle loaded in a matter of a few minutes and Laura backed it out of the garage and onto the highway. Now, it would be only a short while before they would hit the forest in search of the Lair. Laura turned on the radio and began singing along to *Yesterday*, one of her favorite songs. Jim and Red joined in and the threesome headed up Forest Access Road 27, and into the forests of Father Mountain.

At the end of the access road where Jim and Red had stopped before to study the maps, Laura took a hard right turn into the forest.

"Whoa! Where are you going?" Jim asked her.

"This is the old logging road I told you about," she answered. "Glad you brought me along?"

"Yeah, I am," Jim answered. "You'd never know this was a road."

"It'll take us about a mile closer, and leave us with about a mile of hiking to do, but that last mile is rough terrain, and steep," Laura informed them.

Red was happy to hear that they would be a mile closer to their destination before starting their hike, but he wasn't pleased with her last comment. *Rough terrain, and steep*, he thought. *Great, just great.*

Laura took the Cherokee as far as she could in the direction of Lynx Canyon. The trip in, after leaving the graded road, was hairy, to say the least. There were times when Jim and Red were not so sure they wouldn't rather be walking! Not only was the logging road narrow, but it was also rough, and traveled for a while along the extreme edge of some very high cliffs. One wrong move on Laura's part, and they would all be reduced to U.S. Forest Service statistics. Needless to say, Red and Jim were very relieved when Laura announced, "End of the line, boys! This is as close as we get on wheels."

Jim got out of the Cherokee and looked around. There was nowhere to go from the road but up, or down. He knew in his gut that it was *up* they would have to go. Everyone began unloading the gear from the vehicle, sorting it out, and getting situated for the climb.

"Laura, you lead the way. We'll follow," Jim instructed.

Laura gave both boys a sweet smile and headed up the side of the mountain.

"Red, you follow Laura and I'll bring up the rear."

Red smiled a big smile and fell in behind Laura. There was no argument there. Jim followed Red and the trio disappeared into the thick trees. It was steep going and the loose pine needles on the forest floor were poor footing. There was a lot of slipping and sliding, seemingly sliding back one step for every three they took forward. Finally, the slope leveled off a bit and they could stand straight with relative comfort.

They were about twenty-five minutes into the climb when Jim really began to notice the forest around him. He had always thought of the forest as green, but *so many* shades of green he had never imagined. *And*—the smells—*God, what a fragrance*, he marveled! *The photos in the books never smelled like this*, he thought. So far, the only wildlife he had spotted were chipmunks and some birds of some sort. The birds were nothing like he had ever seen at home though, and they were gorgeous.

"Laura. What kind of bird is that, the big gray and white one?" he asked, marveling at a nearby example and pointing to it.

"That's a Clarks nutcracker," she informed him. "Beautiful—aren't they?"

"Yeah, I'll say they are. Pretty neat."

"Laura," Red said, pointing into the trees. "What's that little gray bird called?"

Laura looked in the direction Red was pointing and finally spotted what he was referring to.

"Oh—That's a Canada jay. They're cute little buggers!" she exclaimed.

It was obvious that as many times as she had been up here, she had not lost her fascination with the forest and its inhabitants. She seemed to be just as much in awe of the forest and its wildlife as were the boys.

"We better shove off," Laura finally announced. "Time's a wastin'. We'll be able to see down into Lynx Canyon just over the top of the next rise. That's gonna take your breath away!"

The troop of three marched on, up and up, cresting the rise and gaping at the view before them. It wasn't new to Laura, but it was still breathtakingly beautiful, and a refreshingly relaxing sight, even for her.

The boys, on the other hand, were speechless! The dense green valley below them was indescribable. Oval in shape, it was nestled into the mountain with a precision only God could have dreamed up. From their approach, the floor of the valley sloped down away from them, growing ever deeper, until it reached the back of the valley. There, falling gracefully down the back wall, centered precisely, was a two hundred-foot waterfall. Perhaps only ten feet wide, the falling water had a wispy look to it as updrafts blew water here and there in its attempt to reach the small lake below. The lake had no apparent outlet, but seemed to exist only through a balance of water falling into it and that which could run out through the ground beneath it or evaporate away.

Staring at the sight before him, Jim could not help but wonder why this spot had not yet been spoiled by the tourist trade. *If people got wind of this place, it would be gone in a matter of days*, he thought. *At least as we're seeing it now.*

"What I can't understand, Laura—is why this place isn't swarming with tourists and hikers and campers," Jim pointed out to her. "How did Clermont manage to keep this a secret?"

"Two reasons, Jim," Laura answered. "First, we are a bit off the beaten path when it comes to tourists. Most of them are down in Aspen, Vail, or Estes Park. The second reason is that this is private land, not public. The whole of Father Mountain is owned by a local rancher."

"Lucky guy," Red interjected.

"Yeah, but he made his luck. He came out here from Illinois years ago and scratched out a ranch in the next valley over. He worked it hard and eventually became very wealthy and purchased Father Mountain. Everybody thought he was pretty much crazy, buying a whole mountain and all, but they figured he was probably planning a ski resort or something, or so they speculated. Turns out they were wrong. He never did a thing with it."

"You said he came from Illinois?" Jim asked.

"Yes, Illinois."

"What's his name?"

"Carter Elliott."

Jim's jaw dropped to his chest.

"Red. Did you hear that? Carter Elliott!" Jim exclaimed.

"You don't *know* the name do you?" Laura asked, rather confused at the surprise in Jim's voice.

"Yes, that's the name of the guy who last owned the farm in Illinois where I found the map to the Cats' Lair! That's too amazing. I find a map, hidden—buried in the ground, and it turns out that the guy who owns the destination marked on the map has the same name as the guy who owned the farm where I found it. Coincidence?—I don't think so. Come on, let's get down there and start searching for the Lair!"

The entrance to Lynx Canyon lay about a half-mile ahead and close to five hundred feet below them. It was a pretty easy hike down and into the valley and even Red enjoyed this part of the trip. They found that the ground vegetation was thicker in the valley than it had been up top, probably, because the trees were more sparsely distributed in the valley, allowing more sunlight to reach the ground. Laura led the way to the far edge of the lake where everybody agreed it would be a good place to drop their gear while they scouted the area for a good campsite. The light spray coming from the waterfall was refreshingly welcomed and the sound of the water falling upon the rocks, which formed the foot of the falls, was relaxing.

"This is one cool place," Red commented, sitting down on his backpack. "One fine place!"

Laura and Jim followed Red's lead and took seats on their packs as well.

"Laura—You said you've seen pretty many bobcats up here. Was there any one place where you seemed to see more than anyplace else?" Jim wanted to know.

"Sure. They are thick around the other side of the lake. That's why I brought us to this side to camp. It's not that they are dangerous or anything. If you leave them alone they won't bother you, but they can be pesky when it comes to getting into your food supply while you are away from camp."

"Ever try to see where they go to or come from while you were over there?" Jim asked.

"I never got that close. I didn't want to get them upset by intruding into their little corner over there. This is their valley and I always figured I should probably keep out of the heart of their territory. I would just watch from a distance as they went about their business."

"Okay, but on this trip I think we are going to have to intrude a little. If that is where the most bobcats are, that is probably also where the Lair is. Let's scout out a good campsite for right now, get set for the evening, and tomorrow morning we'll go check out that side of the lake. Sound like a plan to you two?" Jim asked.

"Yep, sounds like a plan to me," Red answered.

Laura smiled and replied, "Me, too. There's a good spot over there a short distance," she said, pointing to a large rock outcropping. "It's behind that large group of rocks, sheltered from this mist and there is plenty of deadwood over there for a fire. It's sort of like a big room, but with no door or ceiling. Come on, I'll show you. It's kinda neat."

Laura headed off in that direction and Red and Jim followed along behind. There was still plenty of daylight left in the day for searching, but tomorrow would be soon enough. Even Jim wanted nothing more right now than to get camped and cook up some food. He was tired and hungry after the exertion required getting up here, and he knew Red felt the same way, two fold.

Laura led them around the leading edge of the rock formation and into exactly what she had described, a rock room. There was plenty of room for their tents and a campfire at a safe distance from them. Other than that, it was quite cozy and confined. The "room" gave Jim a feeling of security, as there was only one direction trouble could come from, not that he expected any, but it was still comforting to think of it that way. Red didn't give it much thought at all, concentrating on gathering wood for the fire. His only thoughts were of supper, and he had already figured out that the fire needed to be built first before he could heat his up.

"Jim, why don't you help Red gather wood and get a fire started while I pitch the tents. Then I have a surprise for you," Laura announced.

"A surprise?" Jim asked.

"Yep. The faster you get that fire going, the faster you'll get your surprise," she stated.

Jim and Red picked up their pace and had a roaring fire going in no time. They had worked so fast that Laura was just barely finishing with the first of the two tents.

"Ready for the surprise, Laura," Red stated, anticipating he knew not what.

"Not ready yet, Red. Help me pitch this second tent first, then I'll get out the surprise," she said, shooting Red a coy smile.

Red turned a little red, blushing at her smile, and rushed over to help out with the tent. Jim noticed Red's enthusiasm for the task and laughed to himself, thinking, *Boy he's got it bad for her! I've never seen him move so fast in my life!* Jim was glad about this development because the quest for the Lair was his bag, not Red's. Red was just along for the trip, a chance to get away from the foundry and see some of the country. Now, he had a reason to be here and that made Jim feel good. *I just hope he doesn't get his heart broken*, he thought.

Laura and Red worked pretty well as a team and had the second tent pitched in a matter of a few minutes. From all outward appearances, it didn't seem like work to them at all. They talked and laughed throughout the whole job, and when they had finished, Laura leaned over and gave Red a little kiss on the cheek.

"Thanks, Red. That was fun," she told him, softly and taking his hand.

"Sure, Laura. No problem. It was my pleasure," he answered, blushing brightly.

Laura released Red's hand and said, "Come on! Time for the surprise!"

She dug into her backpack and pulled out a small cold pack. "STEAK!" she yelled at the top of her lungs. "We've got steak!"

"All—Right!" Jim yelled, equally as loud.

"Awesome!" Red chimed in, smiling from ear to ear.

Jim didn't know what Red had previously planned for his supper, but he knew the T-bone he had just finished, complements of Laura, was a far sight better than the beans and franks he had planned to have. Red was thinking pretty much the same thing about his plans for macaroni and cheese. They were both thinking that bringing Laura along had turned out to be a really good decision.

Red volunteered to clean up the dinner pans and utensils after their meal, but Laura insisted on helping him. Again, there was a lot of laughter involved in the task, which from afar must have sounded more like a party than a chore. Jim just smiled as he listened from inside his tent and began thinking about tomorrow's search for the Lair. He laid back on his sleeping bag and drifted off to sleep to the sound of his friends' laughter.

Red and Laura sat by the fire and talked until the moon, nearly full, was directly overhead. Finally, Laura yawned and told Red she was bushed and needed to get to bed. Red agreed, reluctantly, and started toward his and Jim's tent. Laura reached out and took his hand, smiling at him with the warmest of smiles.

"Red. Keep me company tonight," she said, softly, and blushing slightly looked down at the ground.

"Who? Me?"

"Yes. You. Just keep me company, okay?"

"Sure, Laura. I'll keep you company—anytime."

Laura led the way to her tent and they crawled through the flaps into the beginning of what might grow to become a wonderful relationship. No one was more surprised than Red.

CHAPTER 5

The Lair

*R*ed opened his eyes. Morning had arrived in Lynx Canyon and the first rays of sunlight were beginning to filter through the canvas of Laura's tent. He didn't remember dreaming at all during the night, but this night had been a dream come true in itself. Laura was sleeping peacefully by his side looking even more beautiful in sleep than when she was awake. Red took a deep breath and blew it out slowly through pursed lips. He nudged Laura's arm gently and waited for her eyes to open.

"Good morning," he whispered softly.

"Good morning, Red. Sleep well?" she asked.

"Never better," was his only reply.

"I guess we better get up and make sure Jim doesn't leave without us. He's chomping at the bit over finding the Lair and if we don't get out there we'll probably get left behind," Laura commented, smiling at Red.

Red smiled back and replied, "You've got that right!"

Laura leaned toward Red and gave him another little peck on the cheek.

"Come on, let's find that Lair," she said, and crawled out of the tent.

Red whispered, "Thanks," and followed her.

Of course, Jim was already up and sitting by the remnants of their fire, eating a can of cold beans. Between bites he was studying the valley in apparent consideration of where to begin his search.

"Hey, Jim," Red greeted. "Good morning."

"Good morning to you two, too. How'd you sleep?" he asked, winking at Jim.

"Great, thanks," Red replied.

"Laura?" Jim asked.

"Just fine, Jim. What *are* you eating?" she asked.

"Cold beans—They're great. I didn't feel like building a fire," he said, taking another bite. "I just want to get going. You guys grab something to eat so we can start—okay? I've been studying the valley and I think we should start on the other side of the lake, by the falls, where Laura has seen bobcats in the past. If nothing turns up there we can move along that side of the valley and circle back to here. Sound like a plan?"

"Sounds fine," Red answered.

Laura opened her pack and pulled out a pecan coffee cake.

"Care to join me, Red?" she asked.

Red's eyes lit up.

"Sure! That looks great! It sure beats cold ravioli," he replied, plopping down on the ground beside her. "You're just full of surprises!"

They sat and talked and enjoyed their breakfasts for about a half hour before Jim could stand it no longer.

"You guys ready yet?" he asked, standing and dusting off the seat of his pants.

"I guess we better be," Red said, laughing. "Laura—you ready to go?"

"Ready."

"Okay then. Let's move out," Jim said, motioning toward the falls.

They gathered their packs, hiked them onto their backs, and headed out around the lake. They had no idea what awaited them on the other side, but they were anxious to find out. The Lair would be either a boon or a bust, *if* they found it at all. Part of the fun would be in the looking, but Jim, more than anyone else, hoped for much more.

A more beautiful day for their search could not have been granted. It was a mild morning with a light breeze, which rippled the lake's surface ever so slightly. The early morning sun sparkled in the small waves created there. The sky was a gorgeous deep blue with not a single cloud to be seen.

The trio made their way around the lake and stopped to discuss the best place to begin. Jim pretty much had the say here, but asked Laura's opinion, just the same. She had been here before, after all, and knew where she had previously encountered bobcats. Jim took her up on her suggestion of starting right at the wall of the valley to the side of the waterfall. This had been where she had noticed the most bobcat activity in the past. It only made sense that the name Cats' Lair had come from the proliferation of bobcats in the area, so what they needed to do was pinpoint the source of this activity, if they could.

As Jim rounded a large boulder, he spotted a rather large bobcat, walking toward the valley wall. He raised a finger to his lips and crouched down behind the edge of the rock. Red and Laura stopped, following Jim's lead, and ducked behind the boulder also. Jim watched intently as the cat made its way toward the wall, then disappeared.

"Where the hell did she go?" he murmured under his breath.

"Where did what go?" Red asked, whispering to Jim.

"The bobcat. It was right over there," he stated, pointing toward the sheer rock face of the cliff.

"Maybe she has a den over there—maybe in the ground," Red suggested.

"Well—Let's go find out," Laura said, rising from one knee.

"Yeah—Let's do," Jim replied.

They moved cautiously toward where the cat had vanished, Jim in the lead. He tried very hard to keep his eyes fixed on the exact spot as he stepped over fallen tree trunks and boulders. The spot where the cat had disappeared had been about forty yards away and covering this much broken ground, without looking down at the footing, was extremely difficult. Jim stumbled several times and almost fell once, but his eyes remained locked on the canyon wall.

Arriving at the spot, which Jim was certain he had pinpointed accurately, he saw absolutely nothing. There was nowhere for the bobcat to have gone. He turned to Red and Laura and asked them if they saw anything he was missing. They did not. The cat had simply vanished.

Jim had expected to find a small cave or perhaps a burrow under an old log, but there was absolutely nothing there. The earth came flush with the solid rock wall of the canyon. It was seamless. The rock wall itself was smooth and gray with not so much as a crack in its face.

"What the hell? I don't get it," Jim said, dismayed and confused. "Where the hell could she have gone?"

"Well, maybe you blinked just as she leaped out of your field of sight," Red speculated. "Or maybe you looked away for an instant as she loped off."

"Maybe," Jim said. "But I don't think so. Well—I guess we should go back to that boulder and hunker down and see if another bobcat comes along. Maybe we'll have better luck with the next one."

They all agreed on that plan of action and returned to the large boulder, concealing themselves behind it and settling in to await another cat. They sat in absolute silence for over an hour before Jim broke the silence.

"Laura," he whispered. "Are we in the right place? Or, do you think we would be better off at a different location?"

"No, this is the general area where I have seen the most bobcats. I'd say just hang out here and wait. I've seen as many as five in one day in this area so I don't think we'll have to wait much longer," she explained.

"Okay, we wait," Jim confirmed.

Jim's anxiety was only surpassed by his impatience. He hoped Laura's experiences here in the past would turn out to be the case today. He looked around the forest in all directions and when his eyes fell back to the spot where he had lost the bobcat, there she was again! Jim tapped Laura on the leg and nodded his head in that direction. Laura nodded back in recognition of the cat. They watched as the bobcat proceeded away from where she had previously vanished. She was about to leave the small clearing and enter the forest. *How the hell do you follow a bobcat?* Jim thought to himself. Then, she was gone, disappearing into the trees.

"Now what?" he asked Laura.

"We wait for her to return," Red said, with certainty in his voice. "Then we watch carefully where she goes as she returns."

"What makes you think she'll come back through here?" Jim asked.

"He's right, Jim. Bobcats are no different than us in some respects. They get comfortable with their routines and tend to follow the path of least resistance, just like we do. She probably takes the same route every day, perhaps two or three times a day, coming and going from her den to look for food and satisfy her thirst."

"Well maybe," Jim said. "But the water is behind us, not the way she went," he observed.

"No, there's a stream over in that direction about a quarter of a mile away. She probably hunts and drinks at the stream. The foliage around the stream is thick and probably provides good cover for her to hunt from. Red's probably right. I think she'll come back this way, too."

"Okay, we'll wait—again," Jim replied dryly.

"Patience, Jim. She'll be back," Laura said, patting him on the back.

Laura and Red were right in their assessment of bobcat behavior, or so it seemed, as the bobcat did return, emerging from the exact spot in the forest it had entered two hours before.

Laura was the first to spot her. She nudged Jim with her knee and he turned and saw the bobcat himself, crossing the clearing and heading for the cliff wall. This time he kept his eyes glued on her, not daring to even blink. The cat slowly trotted the length of the clearing and once again, vanished. This time, Jim was certain that he had not faltered in his observation. The cat *did* vanish, and right before his eyes!

       ✤   ✤   ✤

Malic exited the portal to find Damon awaiting him in the windowed chamber. Malic assumed his true form and greeted Damon.

"Ah, Damon. How are you this fine day? Have you been watching the boys?" he asked.

"No, Malic. I have just arrived. You have been outside? What was your assignment?" Damon asked, rather sternly.

"No assignment, Damon. I was just checking on the boys. I went to their camp to see what they were about," he explained.

"And—What *were* they about?"

"I couldn't find them. They were not in their camp and their fire was cold. That is why I returned—to locate them in the window."

"And that is what you should have done from the outset, Malic. That is what the window is for," Damon scolded.

"Yes, Damon. I'm sorry, but I guess I was just curious. I wanted to check on them in person where I could smell their fire and, well—I just wanted to be out there watching them. Can you understand?"

"Yes, Malic, I can understand, but it is risky. You should know that," Damon replied.

"I was the bobcat, Damon. If they were to see me, they would see only a bobcat. Where is the harm in that?"

"The harm in that is not that they might see the bobcat, that is a part of what the bobcat is for, but they might see where the bobcat goes when it returns home. *That* is the danger in what you did, Malic. Perhaps we should locate our friends and see where they are now, wouldn't you agree?"

"Yes, Damon, and I am sorry. I didn't think it through like that."

Malic focused on the window and soon produced the boys and Laura in its view. They were approaching the portal, discussing, much to Malic's dismay, the spot where they had seen the bobcat vanish. Malic turned to Damon who was writing something down on a piece of paper.

"Damon, I am truly sorry. I had no idea."

"You are an aide, Malic. Your senses are not fully developed. That is why you should not venture out unless on assignment and I can monitor you. Now, quickly, take this note and meet the boys if they should enter. Wait in the portal until they enter. There is still the possibility that they will not find it, but they *do* have the map. Drop the note at their feet if they find their way in and return immediately," Damon instructed.

Damon folded the note and when Malic had become the bobcat, placed it in his mouth. Malic bolted for the portal and disappeared into it.

❧   ❧   ❧

Jim approached the wall, slowly and cautiously, not that there was any apparent danger, but because he didn't want to overlook anything that might be a clue. As he drew to within two feet of the cliff, Laura screamed.

"Jim! Stop!"

Jim turned to face her, his heart pounding.

"What?" he asked her; quite nervous about what she had seen that he had not.

"Look down! Your legs…"

Jim looked down toward his feet as directed, his eyes wide, and jumped at least eight feet away, back toward Red and Laura, falling on the seat of his pants as he landed. He looked down and to his horror; his legs were gone from mid thigh, down! He reached down and felt for their presence, but felt only unobstructed air! He could see exposed, the muscles, tendons, bone, and other tissue that comprised his legs where they ended, but there was no pain or bleeding. He looked up at Laura and Jim with a look of total shock and disbelief on his face, and passed out.

Red, totally dumbfounded, rushed to Jim's side, kneeling in the pine needles. He shook Jim but to no avail. He felt for a pulse and it was strong and rapid. Red felt Laura's hand on his shoulder and turned to look into her troubled face.

"He seems to be okay, Laura, other than…"

"I know," she replied, kneeling beside him. "What happened to him, Red? There's no bleeding or anything, just…"

"I think he left his legs in another…another—place. That's what I think," Red stated, trying to put some form of reason to what he had just seen and was still witnessing. "What else could it be? We always thought there was something weird about this Cats' Lair thing. What do you think?"

"I have *no* idea, Red. No idea at all. How did he jump all this way away from there with no legs?" she asked, not knowing what else to say or think.

"I don't think he did jump. I think he was 'thrown' out of there. That's what it looked like to me, like he was shot from there to here! But—what do we do now?"

"Try to wake him, I guess. Then we'll have to try to figure out a way to get him out of here. Maybe build a travois," Laura suggested.

"What about his legs? We've got to get his legs back. Maybe I should crawl in there and try to find them," Red said, not knowing what else was to be done to help his friend. "If it were me I'd want someone to go see if they could be found. Maybe if they were back here with him they would just reattach themselves or something, like nothing had happened at all. I don't know, Laura. Should I try it?" Red asked her, grabbing her hand firmly and holding it tight.

"No! I won't lose you like Jim lost his legs! Forget that idea right now!" she demanded, firmly.

Jim began to stir at that moment and the conversation was dropped to attend to him.

"Jimbo. Shake it off, Jimbo," Red said to Jim, gently patting his cheek.

"I'm awake—What the hell happened? Red, I'm afraid to look. Are my legs still gone?" he asked, hovering on shock and shaking heavily.

"Yeah—They're still gone, but I think I figured out what happened, Jim. Did you jump out of that spot, or were you like—thrown out by some force?" Red asked.

"I was thrown out, hard! I was just standing there and then I was pitched out of that spot like a rag doll. Why?"

"Because I think your legs are in another dimension of some sort. I can't explain it, and I might be totally full of shit, but that's what I think. I also think that one body probably can't exist within both places, so the part of you outside the Lair was propelled out with a great deal of force."

"That sounds hokey, Red. Another dimension? That's like sci-fi crap!"

"You have a better explanation?—I thought not. I want to go in, crawling, so I enter fully into that whatever and find your legs. Maybe if I bring them back here they'll reattach themselves, or at least maybe a doctor can. It's worth a try, right?" Red asked.

"No! Red! It's not worth a try. What if you can't get back? Look what happened to me. It's too dangerous. Just let me rest a while and then *I'll* go in after them. I'll just scoot on in there on my elbows and have a look around. If I don't come back—so what? What have I got to live for now, anyway?" Jim lamented.

"Plenty!" Laura interjected. "You've got plenty to live for, so don't talk like that, Jim. Neither of you are going in there. I'm going to start building a travois and Red and I are going to pull you out of here and back to the Cherokee. Then I'll drive you to the hospital. *That's* what we are going to do!" Laura stated, emphatically. "Got it?"

"Okay, but we are coming back—after I see a doctor and get these stumps bandaged up. Shit! They don't even hurt! But I guess they could get infected the way they are."

Laura and Red went to work cutting the timbers they would need to build Jim's travois. They had only one hatchet, so the work went slowly. No one had brought any twine or rope suitable for lashing the litter together, so Laura set Red to stripping long strands of fiber from beneath the bark of a fir tree, using the strips for lashings. In just under one hour, she had the travois nearly ready for use. Just a few more lashings and they would be able to pull Jim out to the Cherokee.

While Laura and Red had been working on the travois, Jim, relaxing on a bed of pine needles, had fallen asleep. He awoke and reached down to scratch an itch on his shin.

"Hey! Guys! Look! My legs are back!" he yelled at the top of his lungs.

Red and Laura rushed over to him, not comprehending at all what was happening.

"When the hell did they come back?" Red asked, almost as excited for Jim, as Jim was himself.

"I don't know. I fell asleep and when I awoke—they were back!"

"Thank God," Laura said, looking up to the sky above.

"How do they feel?" Red asked.

"They feel fine and they work, too. Look…"

Jim wiggled his toes and rotated his foot while bending his knee.

"It all works just fine!"

"But, can you stand and walk?" Red inquired, appearing a little worried.

"Let's see," Jim said, as he began to stand.

Jim was up in no time and walking about as normally as before the incident had happened.

"Yep! Good as new! And…you know what? Now that we know there is no permanent damage, I vote we crawl into that whatever it is and have a look around."

Jim reached down and picked up a rock about the size of a base-ball and pitched it underhand at the mysterious portal in front of the cliff. The rock fell short, then took one bounce directly into the invisible portal, and disappeared. He picked up another rock and tossed it just left of the first throw and the rock bounced quite nor-mally up against the cliff. Another attempt to the right produced the same results, nothing abnormal.

"Cool! What do you say, Red? You game?" he asked.

"Sure! I'm game!" he answered, then looking at Laura he asked, "If that's okay with you?"

"I don't like it Red, but I can see from your face that there's no stopping you. Just promise me that you'll only stay a short while, on the other side, I mean. I'll be worried to death while you're gone, so don't be gone long, please."

"You can come, too, Laura…" Jim suggested, "If it will make you feel better about this."

"Thanks, Jim, but I think I should stay here until you come out, just in case," she answered.

"Just in case we *don't* come out?" Red asked.

"Yes. Someone has to know where you went—just in case."

"Okay then," Jim said. "Let's go for it! Laura, we'll stay exactly one hour so you'll have an idea when to expect us out. If there's nothing on the other side to see, we'll be back sooner, of course, but if there is something to see over there, we'll be exactly one hour. I'll go first, Red, and you follow right along behind me. The opening appears to be only about three feet wide, so you'll have to follow behind me. Okay? Ready?"

"Ready," Red answered, somewhat sheepishly.

Jim checked his watch and then lowered himself to his hands and knees and approached the portal, staring into it for some clue as to what may lay on the other side. Red got down on all fours also and moved ahead just inches behind Jim. The first thing Red noticed was Jim's head vanishing, then his shoulders, torso, buttocks, legs, and finally, his feet. Jim was gone and he was going. He put his head into the portal and to his amazement Jim reappeared before him! *Cool!* he thought. Red hurried as fast as he could remembering what had happened to Jim when he lingered, part in and part out of the portal. He didn't want to get cut in half, even if he would go back together within an hour or so. The thought of that urged him along quickly.

What the boys found on the other side was a long tunnel. It did not get any larger than the opening had appeared to be, approximately three feet round, the walls of which were gleaming white and smooth as glass, yet soft and warm. Jim stopped about twenty feet in and pressed his hand against the glistening white wall. It gave, ever so slightly, giving him the impression of rubber. There was plenty of light to see by, the light seemingly emanating from the white walls themselves.

Looking ahead, Jim could see no end to the tunnel. It appeared straight; but seemed to just go on indefinitely.

"You doing okay back there, Red?"

"Hell yes! This is cool! What do you see up ahead? All I can see is your nasty ass in front of me!" he laughed.

"Hold on and I'll let you have a look," Jim replied, lying down flat on his stomach so Red could see over him.

"Shit! How the hell far does this thing go?"

"I have no idea. I can't see any end to it either."

"Well, keep an eye on your watch. I don't want to needlessly worry Laura. A half hour in and a half hour out, okay?" Red suggested.

"Sure, Red. That's fine. A half hour in and a half hour out. I'll keep an eye on it," Jim answered.

They were now about fifteen minutes into the tunnel and still there was no end in sight. Jim started up again and then suddenly he stopped. For the first time since entering the Lair he saw something other than white. Up ahead, at quite a distance, he saw something dark in comparison to the surroundings.

"Why are we stopping?" Red wanted to know.

There's something up ahead. I can't make it out yet, but it appears to be moving toward us."

Jim lay down so Red could see.

"Can you make it out?" Jim asked.

"No, but it is moving this way, I think," Red replied. "What should we do?"

"Let's just sit tight and see what it is and what its intentions are. Do you have your hunting knife on you?" Jim asked.

"Yeah."

"Pass it up here, just in case."

Red passed his knife up to Jim who tucked it under his chest, out of sight, but at the ready. He wasn't sure what to expect in here and he was going to be as prepared for whatever may happen as he could be.

The dark figure moved steadily closer.

"Damn, Red. It's a bobcat!"

"I see that now. He must see us by now, too. What should we do?" Red asked, his voice quivering slightly.

"I guess we sit tight. That cat can sure run faster than we can back up. Let's just meet it here and see what happens. Lie down like I am. That's a submissive posture and maybe it won't feel threatened.

Maybe it will just leap right over us and continue on its way—Maybe?"

The bobcat drew to within five feet of Jim's head and stopped. Jim noticed it was carrying something it its mouth, which it finally dropped. As it landed on the floor of the tunnel Jim could see that it was a folded piece of paper. The cat then took one of its front paws and *pushed* the paper toward Jim, then turned and loped away at a slow run. Jim edged forward and picked up the paper.

"What is it?" Red asked, curiously.

"Hold on." Jim studied the opened paper. "It's a note. It says, *'Turn and leave while you are still in your lifetime. The journey you have chosen is double reverse curvilineal. Upon your return, find a way to dispose of the map. It is the sole key to access to and knowledge of this world.'*—What the hell does that mean?"

"I have no idea, but I think we'd better heed its advice and get the hell out of here," Red suggested. "It doesn't sound good, whatever it means. Come on, I'm turning around and heading back."

"Go. I'm right behind you. We've been in here thirty minutes anyway. Let's get back to Laura before she gets too worried."

A half an hour later, when the boys should have emerged from the tunnel, the end was nowhere in sight. They continued crawling until they were exhausted and stopped to rest. Their outbound journey had now lasted six hours and still the opening to the outside world was not visible.

They discussed the possibility that in all the whiteness they may have made a turn from the main tunnel into some adjoining passage. They dismissed the notion after a short discussion about the possibility. *Double reverse curvilineal? Was this what the note had meant?* they wondered.

After a short rest, they pushed on down the white tube, staring ahead for any sign of the exit. It was not in sight. Eight more hours passed and they seemed no closer to exiting this place than they had been fourteen hours ago.

"Damn, Red. I'm exhausted. I've got to stop and get some sleep," Jim said, collapsing to the tunnel floor. "My back is killing me and my hands and knees are raw."

"Mine, too. Let's sleep a few hours and give our backs a break," Red agreed.

They slept, restlessly, but they slept. Six hours later, they resumed their retreat from this hell they had willingly entered. They had now been twenty hours in this place, this tunnel, and they were beginning to feel quite claustrophobic. Eight more hours of crawling found them nowhere. They were becoming dehydrated and with the lack of any features other than an all-enveloping whiteness, they were becoming disoriented. There was no up and there was no down. There was only white, *everywhere*. It was not hot and it was not cold. The temperature in the tunnel seemed to be a function of whatever made you not notice it at all. Pain existed, however, and they felt it acutely.

After another eight hours, thirty-six in all, Red saw something ahead other than whiteness.

CHAPTER 6

The Wait

*D*amn, Red, *it's been over two hours now. Where are you guys?*
Laura thought to herself, worrying about the boys. Two hours
had passed since they entered the Lair and they were now an hour
late in returning.

Laura was growing more anxious now with each minute that
passed. When their failure to return had passed the one-hour over-
due point, she had decided that something must be wrong. Prior to
then, she had just considered the boys caught up in the excitement of
exploring a new place, letting the time get away from them. *Come on
guys, where are you? Please come out of there...*she thought, anxiously.

Once their tardiness reached two hours, Laura decided to head
back to camp and wait there. The boys would know where to find
her and she needed to get a drink and eat a little something. Hiking
around the lake her thoughts remained on Red and what might have
happened to him in that place. As much as she didn't like thinking it,
she was frightened, and was now sure that Red had been injured or
worse. *What if he's trapped in there and can't come out? What if
he's...no, Laura, don't even think that!*

Back at camp she restlessly rummaged through her pack looking
for something to eat, but nothing looked good to her now. She

pulled out a small snack cake and sitting by the remains of their fire, nibbled on it, trying to get comfortable on the hard ground. She racked her mind for the answer to her most pressing question, *What do I do now? Wait. Just wait. What else can I do?*

Laura sat by the cold fire and waited…and waited, until dark was upon her. She did not relish the idea of staying the night alone, not under these circumstances. She had done it many times before, but now, there was something different about sleeping out in the forest. Something different and ominous was hanging over this night's stay. *God, where are the boys? Where's Red?*

Daylight arrived none to soon and she began hiking to the Lair without bothering to eat. When she arrived, she sat on the forest floor and stared at the Lair. *Maybe I should go in after them. Maybe I can be of some help.* "No Laura," a voice in her head cautioned. "Forget that idea," it said. *Yeah, you're right,* she thought. *Go get the sheriff and some rescue people,* she thought to herself, and standing, headed back around the lake at a jog.

Rather than go back to camp, Laura headed straight out of the canyon and up the ridge. Cresting the top, she looked back for a moment, and then headed down to her Cherokee. She was soon on the highway and Clermont was only minutes away. *How am I going to explain this to the sheriff,* she wondered. *I'll just tell him the truth and show him when we get up there,* she decided. "That'll be best," she said aloud, wondering if it truly would.

Laura entered the sheriff's office with a great deal of apprehension about the story she was about to tell. Perhaps a gentle softening of the facts would be better accepted by the sheriff and met with a little less skepticism.

"Hi, Maria. Is the sheriff in?" Laura asked "I need to see him about a serious matter."

"Hola, Miss Palmer. No, he's over at Teufel's getting a new key made for the office. Can I help you?"

"No thanks, Maria. I'll just run over there and talk with him. That's on Euclid, right."

"Sí, that's it," Maria directed.

"Thanks, Maria," Laura replied, as she went back out onto the sidewalk. She started walking toward Teufel's Hardware, which was only a block and a half away, revising her story in her mind as she walked. *Soften the truth,* she thought.

Upon entering Teufel's she immediately heard the sound of the key-grinding machine and looked in that direction. Jim Teufel was grinding a key as Sheriff Cramer watched with all the attention given a dying man's confessions.

"Sheriff Cramer," Laura interrupted. "Can I talk with you a minute?"

"Sure, Miss Palmer. What can I do for you?" Sheriff Cramer asked, smiling handsomely.

"I have a problem. I met these two really nice guys from Illinois the other day and we went camping up in Lynx Canyon."

"Nice area," the sheriff interjected. "What's the problem?"

"Well, they found this sort of cave and decided to explore it. That was yesterday morning. They never came back out. I'm afraid they're stuck in there, or worse," she said, a tear forming at the bottom of her right eye.

"There, there, Laura. Don't worry yourself like that. They probably went in so far they decided to sleep the night in the cave. They're probably up there in the canyon looking for you right now," he said, trying to comfort Laura as best he could.

"But they promised to come out in an hour. I don't think Red would stay in there all night and worry me like that," she explained.

"Sounds to me like you're rather fond of this Red fellow," Sheriff Cramer commented.

"Yes, I am—and I'm worried about him."

"Okay, missy. I'll tell you what. We'll just go up there and have a look. I'll get Lou and a few of the boys and we'll go up there and see if we can find them in there."

"Thanks, Sheriff!" Laura exclaimed, a huge smile bursting upon her face.

"You'll have to lead us in there though. I've never run across a cave up in Lynx, so I have no idea how to find it."

"Sure, I'll take you straight there. When can we leave?" Laura asked, anxiously.

"You give me an hour to get organized and then meet me at my office. We'll leave straightaway from there. How's that sound?"

"Sounds great, Sheriff, and—thanks again!"

Laura left Teufel's, deciding to go by the Hummingbird for a bite to eat. After she had gone, the sheriff scratched his head, a perplexed look on his face.

"I've never heard tell of any cave up in Lynx Canyon, Sheriff," Jim said.

Pete Cramer looked at Jim and replied, "Me neither, Jim. Wonder what she's talking about, anyway? You don't suppose there could be a cave up there—do you?"

"I've hiked every inch of that valley deer and elk hunting. I never ran across one," Jim replied. "I'd be damned surprised if there turned out to be one there."

Laura half-heartedly ate a light lunch and departed for Sheriff Cramer's office. She found the sheriff ready to go, and he had recruited Lou Long and the Merkle brothers, Roy and Rick, for the trip. Laura led the way out to 27 and up to the old logging road, where they parted with their vehicles.

The rescue party, with Laura in the lead, hiked on in to Lynx Canyon.

"Sheriff. I want to check our camp first, just in case they did come back out. They could be waiting there if so," Laura advised.

"Sure, missy, lead the way."

The camp proved empty and just as Laura had left it. It didn't appear that anyone had been there since she had left it several hours before. Laura led the party away, around the lake and in the direction of the Lair. She stopped ten feet short of the portal and pointed.

"It's right there, Sheriff. You can't see it, but it's right there in front of the cliff."

Sheriff Cramer craned his neck and stared to where Laura was pointing. He saw absolutely nothing but a sheer rock wall.

"Where?" he asked. "I don't see any cave, or even a crack in that wall."

"In front of the wall, Sheriff. Watch. I'll show you."

Laura looked around and found a small rock about the size of a tennis ball. She pitched it, underhand, at the portal. The rock bounced, and then rolled up against the face of the cliff. Laura stared at it as it came slowly to rest. She scrambled about searching for another rock, and coming up with one, tried again.

When this stone came to rest almost next to the previous one, Sheriff Cramer removed his hat, and scratching the back of his head, asked, "Laura. What on Earth are you trying to do?"

"I'm throwing the rocks into the Lair, but they're not disappearing like Red and Jim did."

Her voice was shaking and she was obviously very upset, but to Pete Cramer it sounded like she was just plain incoherent, *a bit touched* came to mind as he thought about it.

"Miss Palmer—There's obviously no cave here. Are you sure this is the right spot?" Lou asked.

"Yes, this is the right spot and it wasn't really a cave, like you'd think of, anyway. I didn't know what else to call it. It was more like an invisible opening into another dimension or something. That's what Red thought, anyway."

"You mentioned the Lair a moment ago. What was that in reference to?" the sheriff asked.

"Jim and Red had a map to a place called the Cats' Lair. That's what they came to Colorado to find—to this valley. We found it, just like the map said, and they went in—yesterday!"

Laura became silent and dropped to the ground, sitting cross-legged and staring into the Lair. She could hear the muffled conversation of the sheriff, Lou and the Merkle brothers behind her, but none of it was registering in her mind. She *knew* what they were saying—*That girl needs help, Sheriff—Touched, if you ask me—Plain crazy is what I'd call her...*

Laura slowly leaned to her right and came to rest on her elbow, forehead resting in palm and began to cry. Sheriff Cramer bent down and helped her to her feet.

"Come on, missy. Let's get you home where you can get some rest," he comforted her.

Lou led the way out of Lynx Canyon, the sheriff and Laura behind him with Roy and Rick Merkle bringing up the rear. The sheriff drove Laura home and saw her into the house while Roy parked her Cherokee in the garage.

Sheriff Cramer got the boys' names from Laura and the fact that they were from Illinois. That's all she could really tell him about them. He put it on the wire as two missing persons, but didn't really expect anything to ever come of it. That much was his duty, but believing the whole story was optional, and he did not, not for a minute.

Laura let a day pass by before returning to their campsite in the canyon. She waited in camp the entire day, but neither Red, nor Jim ever came. She came back daily for nearly two weeks, and then only once every two weeks. Finally, after three months, she broke down their camp and hauled away the tents and gear a little at a time and stowed it all in her garage.

Several more months passed before she could bring herself to go back to the Lair. When she did, she took along three large burlap bags, triple lining them within each other, and a Have-a-Heart trap, a large one, large enough to trap a bobcat. By morning the next day she had caught her first cat.

She hauled the bobcat back to her house in the burlap sack. She had constructed a large pen in the backyard where she released her first hope. She knelt down outside the fencing and called to the cat.

"Red. Red, is that you? Where's you buddy, Jimbo? Don't worry, I'll find him for you."

✿   ✿   ✿

Damon watched Laura with a tear in his eye. This tragedy, the result of the boys meddling where they weren't intended to go, was indeed a sad development. He turned away from the window, just as Malic came through the falls.

"Hello, Damon," Malic greeted. "What are you watching in here all these hours. I have been looking everywhere for you."

"I've been watching Laura. Pity what has become of her. It is sadder than even I can comprehend. And—All because of those meddlesome boys."

But Damon knew that he bore some of the responsibility for Laura's plight. His intervention to elicit her story of Little Hawk had unwittingly led to her participation in the boys' quest. For a Guardian, whose purpose it was to aid the Kinder, this was a heavy and smothering burden to carry.

"The boys didn't intend for this to happen, Damon. Especially Red. I believe he was growing very fond of her. He would be heartsick if he could see her now."

"Yes, Malic, I'm sure he would be," Damon answered, feeling a very similar feeling in his own heart.

CHAPTER 7

The Escape

"**J**im! I think I see the end of the tunnel! I see something ahead! God, let it be the end of this damn tube!"

Red picked up the pace as much as his tired and aching body would allow. Jim accelerated also, staying right on Red's heels. Thirty-six and a half hours after entering the Cats' Lair, they emerged into the forest of Father Mountain. Laura was nowhere to be seen.

It was daylight, but it was cold. Not bitter cold, but it was not the warm summer morning they had left a day and a half ago.

"Damn!" Red shouted. "Laura's probably scared to death for us. Let's get back to the camp and find her. She's going to kill us for being gone so long!"

They tried to stand and found that their bodies were not cooperative in the effort. Every muscle in their backs screamed with pain when they tried, but they managed to get erect and painfully hobbled off toward the lake's edge where they quenched their searing thirst before starting back to camp.

"Red. You notice how chilly it is?" Jim asked.

"Yeah. A front must have moved in while we were in there. It is a bit chillier than when we left, but Laura will probably have a good fire going. Let's hurry."

They rounded the lake and entered the rock room, which had served as their campsite, but there was no sign of Laura or their equipment.

"Damn! She's not here!" Red cried out. "Where could she be?"

"And where's all our stuff?"

"She must have packed it all up and hauled it back with her. But why? Why didn't she just wait for us here?" Red questioned.

Jim thought for a moment.

"She probably waited for us until the following morning, then probably packed up and went for help," Jim speculated, trying to settle Red down and alleviate his fears. "Look, it's getting near dark. Let's build a fire and camp out here for the night. It's sheltered and the fire will keep this little room pretty warm if we build it big and keep it fueled. Hell, Laura will probably return with help before dark, but if we leave now, dark will catch us in this forest with no shelter at all."

"Yeah, you're right. I guess it would be best to just stay here. I wish we at least had a couple of frickin' sleeping bags though. This sucks!"

They went about gathering firewood and clearing the ground of rocks and pebbles where each planned to sleep. It wouldn't be the most comfortable of nights, but they'd survive. The only good thing about the past day and a half was that Jim had half a book of matches in his pocket. They built a large, blazing fire, which warmed up the small area nicely. They lay down in their chosen spots and stared at the fire.

"This isn't so bad, Red. It could be worse," Jim encouraged, noticing the glum look on his friend's face.

"No, not so bad, but I'd rather see Laura and a rescue party walk through that opening right now. Besides, I'm starving! We haven't eaten since yesterday morning. *That* sucks, big time!"

Jim pulled from his shirt pocket the note Malic had dropped before him in the portal.

"I guess we found out what this note means by *double reverse curvilineal*," Jim offered.

"Yeah, what's that?" Red asked.

"That it takes a whole hell of a lot longer to get out of the Lair than it does to get in. That's what."

"I think we found out what *reverse curvilineal* means, but not the double part," Red responded.

"Why's that?"

"Because *double* had nothing to do with the time it took to get out. It took us a day and a half to get back out from a half hour's trip in. *That* ain't double!" Red said, philosophically. I think curvilineal means the tunnel curves, and—there are *two* tunnels—the one in and the one out. Hell, we thought we were going straight, but in there, how can you tell? You can't, and one tunnel, the one going out is a hell of a lot more curved than the one going in. That's what I think it means, anyway."

"We were always in the one tunnel. How can the same tunnel be curved so that it has a different length when traveled one way as opposed to the other? It makes no sense," Jim argued.

"Maybe the curve is in time, not in the tunnel itself. Maybe our perception of moving normally through the tunnel on the way out was stilted. Like, time wise, for every one step we made on the way out, we had made sixty steps on the way in," Red tried to explain, noticing the baffled look on Jim's face. "Put it like this—Our brains slowed down until our perception was like that of an alligator's on a cold morning, unable to perceive movement in his surroundings because of slowed brain function. I read about that once. Maybe our brains were somehow slowed down like that so that we *only thought* we were moving normally when in fact we were moving at a creakingly slow pace."

Jim thought about that for a moment, and then asked, "Who the hell wrote the note? Whoever it was probably saved our lives. If we had gone on we would probably have died of thirst before we ever got back out. Think about that a minute," Jim suggested.

Jim glanced back down at the note.

"The note says that we should 'dispose of the map.'"

"Then do it," Red said, emphatically. "Just do it for Christ's sake."

Jim took the map from his shirt pocket and tossed it into the fire, along with the note. The note flared up and vanished in a matter of a second or two, but the map drifted up on the convection currents from the fire and fluttered away, unscathed. Jim jumped up and retrieved it from where it had settled to the ground and wadded it up into a ball, throwing it back into the center of the fire.

Silence fell between the two boys as each tried to understand, in his own way, what had happened to delay their return to camp for so long. An inexplicable curve in the tunnel, curves in time, super-slowed perceptions—black magic—were among the possibilities covered in each of the boys' thoughts. Neither could make total sense of the whole of it, only the one fact that it had *somehow* taken thirty-six hours to travel *straight* out of a place it had taken a half hour to travel into. That was the one reality they understood.

Fatigue dictated sleep, and Red and Jim fell asleep by the fire each thinking his own thoughts of the previous day and a half. There would be no more conversation or speculation between them this night. Sleep was upon each in a matter of minutes.

Jim awoke at daybreak, shivering from the cold. He and Red had slept so soundly that neither had awakened to add wood to the fire and it had died to embers during the course of the night. He scrambled to add wood to the fire, which burst into a welcomed blaze, almost instantly, as the dry wood fell upon the glowing coals. He huddled close, knees folded to his chest and reached back to nudge Red awake.

"Red, get up and move closer to the fire before you freeze to death," he instructed, as Red's bleary eyes opened. "It's frickin' cold out here!"

Red noticed instantly upon awakening and without speaking a word, moved close to the fire, rubbing his hands over his legs and arms in an attempt to get his circulation going.

"Crap! It's colder than a well-digger's ass out here!" Red complained. "It's supposed to be frickin' July, not November!" he added.

Red's last comment got Jim thinking and he looked out the opening of their rock room to a nearby aspen tree. The leaves were still green, assuring him that it could not be November. But that didn't mean that it wasn't late September or early October. He thought about that for a moment, and then dismissed the notion as quickly as he had entertained it. *That's impossible,* he thought. *It's just a cold front,* he reasoned, satisfying his confusion with the only explanation that made any sense at all.

"Laura never came back last night," Red pointed out to Jim.

"Yeah, I noticed."

"Maybe she'll be back this morning with some help," Red speculated.

"Maybe, but I'm not waiting. I'm heading out of here as soon as I warm up a bit. I'm hungrier than hell and I just want to get back to the Jeep, get something to eat, and find a nice warm motel room."

"Maybe Laura will put us up for a day or two," Red said. "And—cook us up some grub!"

"Maybe she will. That would be fine by me. Let's get off this damn mountain and find out. Are you ready to travel?"

"Ready as I'll ever be—Let's move out."

They stood and as Jim began to kick dirt over the fire to smother it, he noticed the wadded map resting among the glowing embers of the fire. He reached in and carefully picked it out, unfolding it as he did. To his amazement, the map was perfectly smooth, like it had never been wadded up at all. There was not a single crease or fold mark upon it.

"Damn, Red. It didn't burn. It isn't even singed!" he said, in total disbelief. "And—look. There isn't a crease in it!"

"Well, try tearing it into little pieces and throw them in there," Red suggested.

Jim tried to do as Red had suggested, but the map would not tear. He used all his might to try to get a tear started, even using his teeth to initiate one, but to no avail. It simply would not be torn. He took Red's hunting knife and drove it through the map and pulled down cutting the map, but the map sealed itself together above the blade, immediately, as the blade passed on. Jim stared at Red and shrugged, folding the map and placing it back in his shirt pocket.

"I think I know now why this damn map was buried in that jar, Red," Jim stated.

"Yeah, me too."

"When I get back home, I am going to put the damn thing right back where I found it. That's what I'm going to do," Jim said.

"If I were you, I'd put it in a box, fill it with concrete and drop it in the ocean. *That's* what I'd do with it!" Red exclaimed, in no uncertain words.

The boys kicked dirt over the fire until it was smothered out, and then walked to the lake where they each drank as much as they could hold for the trip down the mountain. It was about twenty miles back to Laura's house, over seven hours of hiking and walking. They hoped they might get lucky and be able to hitchhike a ride once they hit the highway, but that was not a certainty. They needed to fill up on water for the long, dry walk back.

When each had drank his fill they began. First they would have to hike up and out of Lynx Canyon to the ridge above it, and then down to the access road. This would be the hardest part of the journey, climbing and hiking over rough ground, but once back to the access road it would simply be one *long* walk.

Thirty minutes after leaving the lake they found themselves on top of the ridge, looking down toward the forest road. They were shivering again as the warmth from their fire had left them. It was a sunny morning, but the warm rays of the sun could not benefit them beneath the thick forest canopy. Jim explained to Red, who was complaining profusely about the cold, that once they reached the access road they would be in the warmth of the sunlight. Red seemed to accept Jim's words of comfort and took the lead, moving quickly down the steep slope toward the road.

Another half-hour had passed as they emerged from the forest onto the gravel road. It was bathed in sunlight and the radiant heat from its warm glow quickly improved the boys' outlook. Had it been a cloudy day, Jim felt that Red might have lost what little composure he had remaining, for he had feared during the last leg of the trip that Red was about to become unglued. Red had a very low threshold for discomfort and pain, and it had been showing as they had crested the ridge. Jim was thankful for the sunlight for Red's sake, more so than for himself.

They began their walk down the access road toward the highway, each hoping and praying to see Laura's red Cherokee coming toward them as they negotiated each bend in the road. With each bend in the road came another disappointment. As they completed each curve there was no Laura and there was no highway in sight. *Maybe around the next bend,* they thought. *Maybe the next bend…*

It was early afternoon when they rounded the final bend and spotted the highway stretched out below them. It was the most welcomed sight they had come to hope for. The fact that Laura had not come looking for them was disheartening and worried them, especially Red. Red was beginning to worry that something bad had happened to her while they were, wherever they were, in that damned Lair. He couldn't understand how she could simply leave and not come back looking for them. They had been separated only two and a half days, surely not long enough to give up on him. There should be search parties and helicopters swarming the area. Then the reality of the situation hit him square in the face. *What if she told them the truth?*

Red stopped in his tracks and turned to face Jim.

"What if Laura told the authorities the truth, Jim?" he asked, sweat forming in beads on his forehead. "They would never have believed a story like that. That's why there is no one looking for us."

Jim, who had been trying to make sense of the same question, commented, "Yeah, I thought of that, too. But even if she did actually tell them the whole truth, and they didn't believe her, that doesn't explain why *she* isn't out here looking for us. It's like she vanished as well. You don't suppose she came in the Lair looking for us—do you?"

"Shit! I never even thought of that!"

They moved to the edge of the road and sat down under a large pine to rest and discuss the matter. Red put his hand on his whiskered chin and began rubbing it, a sign Jim understood to mean that Red was thinking hard.

"No, she didn't follow us in there," he stated, after several minutes of deliberation. "If she had, she would probably still be in there, having entered after us. That doesn't necessarily mean that we would have run into her in there either. That's a weird place and who knows what the rules are? No, if she went in there and is still in there, our camping gear would still be at the campsite and her Cherokee would still be parked up the road. She left, Jim. I'm convinced of that—But why didn't she come back? That's what befuddles me. What could have happened to her?"

"Maybe nothing happened, Red. Maybe she did come back and search and wait the whole next day. Maybe she had just gone home right before we came out last night. Maybe she couldn't get out of work today, for some reason, to come back and wait again today. After all, it's not like we were lost. She knew *where* we were, and how was she going to explain that to the authorities?"

"She would have tried. I know she would. Work's not a problem either. Alice is covering her shifts all week remember? She could have, and would have insisted that the sheriff come along with her to see what she was talking about, even if he didn't believe her. She would have taken him to the spot and demonstrated—maybe—by throwing a rock into the Lair, like you did. She would have insisted upon at least that much cooperation from him. I know it, Jim."

Jim thought for a moment, and then offered another explanation.

"Remember what the note said, that the map was the sole key to knowledge of and access to the Lair? Maybe she did come back with the sheriff and all. Maybe she did try to show them what she was talking about. Maybe, just maybe, without the map in her possession, the Lair couldn't be found. Maybe that is why no one has ever accidentally stumbled across it. Maybe that's the secret to its staying undiscovered over time. The map is the key, the *only* key, to opening the gate. It has to be present for the phenomena to appear."

"Maybe, but then there must be more than one map if you are going to tie the crazy Indian into this theory," Red postulated.

Not necessarily. Maybe he was with the farmer from Illinois. Maybe he was the farmer's guide into the Father Mountain area. They may have gone in together," Jim suggested.

"Nope, won't work," Red said. "The Indian came out babbling about Grover Cleveland being President. That was sometime in the late 1800's, I think. The farmer was looking for the Lair, according to Gillespie, in 1930. The times are all wrong. There must be at least two maps if you are right about it being the only key to access to the Lair. And—if you are right, that proves that Laura could not have followed us in there. We went in together, but once we were in there she would probably be locked out, so to speak."

"Okay, so we are assuming that you need the map, a map, to gain access. The Indian has a map and he goes in sometime in eighteen hundred and something. The farmer goes into the Lair in 1930. The farmer exits in 1990 and the Indian comes out in 1998. That means that the Indian was in there at least thirty years before the farmer and remained in there eight years after the farmer had gone. That's ninety-eight years, at least! Going by our experience, the Indian would have never survived. For that matter, the farmer was in there sixty years. He too, would have died from lack of food and water. None of this makes any sense to me. Compound that with the fact that both of them were young men when they emerged, not old like the dates would indicate they should be. It makes absolutely no sense at all."

"Forget the dates, Jim. You're getting off track. What about the map, or maps? That is what we are trying to figure out now. Is there more than one, or not? Or—do we even care?" Red asked.

"Yes. I care. I want to know what the hell we have been dealing with, and understand it. Don't you? Look—There is one explanation that gets both the Indian and the farmer in there with just one map. I think that the Lair has been up there on Father Mountain for all time. I think the Indians have known about it for quite some time, perhaps several hundred years. I think some medicine man or some-one like that, with mystical powers, created the map using French he had learned from some explorer. He put some sort of spell on it to make it the sole key to knowledge of the Lair."

"That's nuts," Red interjected.

"Let me finish, Red. Then, sometime in the late 1800's the young teenage Indian gets curious and takes the map from the sacred place where it was kept by the medicine man. He goes to the spot and walks in—like I did. When he looks down he notices his legs are missing and freaks, dropping the map just outside the portal. Unlike me, he knows his legs are apparently gone and drops, falling com-pletely into the portal. Once in there his legs are back and he settles down a bit. He decides to follow the tunnel and see where it takes him, but no bobcat comes with a note to warn him as quickly as one did for us. He goes in much further than we did and it takes him damn near a hundred years to get out."

"This is the craziest story I have ever heard," Red said, breaking in again.

"I'm not done. The map is indestructible, as we found out, and it survives up there on the mountain, blowing about to where it was finally found by the farmer who had come to the area to start a new life in the west. This was in 1930. He had just come out to Colorado to look for land and was out exploring the possibilities. He finds the map and gets curious about it, asking folks about it at the café and all. That's when he met Gillespie the first time. He finally finds the Lair after searching for a while, and enters. He too, goes in much deeper than we did and he doesn't emerge for sixty years. He tries to destroy the map, but finds that it can't be done, so while back in Illinois settling his business, he buries the map where I found it figuring that no one would ever find it there. He *thinks* that he has ended the madness permanently. When he gets back to Colorado and eventually becomes very successful and wealthy, he buys the mountain, just in case. He wants to control what happens there and make sure that it doesn't become developed or anything like that."

"Wait! Red yelled, waving his hands in front of Jim. "Just stop there—please. That's a great story, but it's all made up in your head. As good as it sounds on the surface, it still doesn't explain how they survived in there all those years. It all fits, except for that," Red informed Jim.

"Well—Maybe you can't actually die in there, Red. We weren't in there long enough to find out, now were we?"

Red had no answer for that, but his mind was on his stomach, more so than on Jim's fantastic explanation. All he wanted to do was go find Laura and get something to eat. As far as he was concerned, the explanations could wait until after that had been accomplished. He told Jim as much and they started again toward the main highway below. Thirty minutes later they had reached their destination.

They took a short breather, and then turned up the highway in the direction of Clermont. It was seven miles to town, but they planned to stop at Laura's house on the outskirts and see if she was home and hopefully, get something to eat there.

Their hope of hitching a ride to Laura's waned with each mile they traveled. The highway, not generally heavily traveled, was totally deserted so far today, not a single car having passed them in the first three miles of their journey. This, in itself, didn't surprise them. They remembered on their few drives out to and from the access road that there had been no traffic to speak of then, either. Why should today be any different, when it meant something?

They pushed on, weary and hungry, the thought of a hot meal keeping them focused on the task at hand. Finally, Jim spotted something coming toward them. The vehicle was coming from the direction of Clermont, so it wouldn't help them hitch a ride to town, but it was good to see the first sign of life after nearly six miles on the highway.

As expected, the vehicle whisked by at about seventy miles per hour and disappeared around the last bend behind them.

"What the hell was that?" Red asked astonished by what he had just seen.

"I have no idea!" Jim answered, still staring down the road where the vehicle had disappeared from view. "I've never seen anything like *that* before! There must be some fancy car show nearby, or something."

"It didn't have any wheels or tires, Jim! It was *floating on air!* What's with that?"

"I don't know, but I've seen boats that operate like that, on a cushion of air. I guess that guy just applied that technology to his show car. Kinda cool if you ask me!" Jim answered, in awe of the car.

"Huh—fancy," Red said. "Let's get moving. It can't be more than a mile or so to Laura's by now. My stomach is growling like crazy.—Hey!" Red exclaimed as he reached into his hip pocket. "My Hershey Bar! I forgot all about it!"

Red opened the wrapper and bit into the candy bar with all the fervor of a lion chomping into a gazelle. "Damn!" he hollered. "This thing's as hard as a rock!"

Jim took the candy from Red and examined it. Where Red had bitten into it, there was barely a tooth mark. He tried to break the bar in half and it snapped with the sound of a firecracker.

"Damn! That *is* stale!" he commented. "When did you buy this?"

"Just the other day, while I was waiting for you in the Jeep. I bought two from a kid while you were in the diner. I ate the other one then—it was fine."

Jim stared at the candy bar again and replied, "Well, I'd say he screwed you on this one."

Jim and Red began walking toward Laura's house once again, but the candy bar remained on Jim's mind. There was a lot more than a couple of day's age on it, and he could come up with no explanation for it. He tossed it by the side of the road and shrugged his shoulders. *The kid probably saved it over from last year's fund-raiser,* he thought, coming to the only conclusion that made sense.

They saw no more traffic along the way and as they rounded a bend in the road, Jim froze on the spot.

"Red—Did we go the wrong way back at the end of the access road?" he asked, confused at what lay before him.

"No. I don't think so. We turned right—that was right."

"But, Laura's house was the last house on the edge of town. *That's not Laura's house!*"

Jim was looking at a two-story, colonial, sitting on the side of the road where Laura's house should have been. Or at least, the colonial shouldn't have been there as Laura's should have been the first house they would come to. Beyond that colonial, Jim could see at least two more.

"Where the hell is Laura's ranch?" he asked Red, as much as asking himself.

"Maybe it's on down aways. Maybe we aren't to town yet. Maybe we just never noticed these houses out here when we were driving. I don't know," Red offered, as confused as was Jim.

"Okay, let's say we never noticed them while driving and keep going. Laura's can't be far then. I hope."

The boys walked on, passing the colonial homes, and soon came to Laura's ranch house. The problem though, was that the "new" colonials did continue all the way to Laura's house. There were seven, to be exact, and Laura's house was no longer the *last* house on the outskirts of town!

"Damn, Red. Are you as confused as I am?" Jim asked his friend.

"Absolutely!" came the response.

"I don't get it. Where did these new houses come from?"

"Nothing has gone right since going into the Lair. What did you expect, Jim? Don't question it or you'll just get more confused. Let's just go up to the door and knock and hope Laura's home."

"My Jeep is gone," Jim said, in a matter of fact tone. "We left it right there on the drive and now it's gone."

"Great! That probably means Laura's not home. She probably took it into town on an errand or something. Just great!" Red complained. "Now we'll have to wait on her to get some grub in us."

"I don't know, Red," Jim said, looking into the open garage. "Look in the garage. It's empty. If she took my Jeep, her Cherokee would be in the garage—It's not!"

"Come on, let's knock and see for ourselves," Red stated. "We won't get any answers standing out here."

Red was the first to the door and rapped heavily on it with his knuckles. There was a momentary silence, then the door opened to reveal a middle-aged woman of oriental descent. She smiled and greeted the boys.

"Hello. May I help you?" she asked.

"Ah—Yes—We're looking for Laura, Laura Palmer," Red said, hesitantly.

"Laura?—Palmer?—Oh, you must mean the crazy old lady that once lived here. She has been deceased for years," the lady informed them.

"No. You don't understand. Laura is about twenty or twenty-one years old. Pretty, with blonde hair. You know—Laura..." Red tried to clarify himself.

"I'm sorry, but the only people who live here are myself and my husband. The only Palmer I know of was the old lady who used to live here some ten years ago or so," she insisted.

"Why did you refer to her as '*the crazy old lady*'?" Jim asked, starting to put a few things together.

"Because she kept bobcats here. Many, many bobcats. She trapped them in the mountains and kept them in a large pen out back."

"That's eccentric, but not crazy," Jim replied.

"Yes, eccentric, but naming them all 'Red' is crazy," she replied. "Wouldn't you say so? And—She talked to them! All of them! '*Come here, Red*.' she would say. '*That's a good boy. Where's your friend, Jimbo?*' she would ask, over and over again. I heard her when we came to look at this place. She was being moved into a nursing home at that time. I heard that she had passed away a year or so later. What a shame, the poor woman."

Red and Jim just stared at each other, mouths agape.

"Was she your grandmother?" the lady asked. "I'm sorry. I didn't think about that. I'm sorry to have spoken of her rudely, but those are the facts as I know them."

"No," Red replied, finally. "A friend."

"I'm sorry," she replied. "And you were unaware of her passing?"

"Yes, we were unaware," Jim answered, in a total cloud of confusion. "What's the date?" he asked.

"October twentieth."

"What year?" Red asked, sensing where Jim's thoughts were going.

"2086, of course," she replied.

❧   ❧   ❧

Damon entered the windowed room to find Malic standing stiff, head lowered, looking at the floor. He hadn't noticed Damon's arrival and Malic appeared to Damon to be involved in some deep and troublesome thought.

"Malic. Are you all right?" he asked, concerned for his aide.

"No, Damon. My heart is very heavy. The boys have now discovered what has happened to them and Red is extremely sad and upset."

"Then he knows?" Damon asked.

"Oh, yes. He knows. The boys have talked with the lady who now lives in Laura's old house and she has told them the story," Malic replied.

"Does she know about them?" Damon asked, clearly concerned about that possibility.

"No. The boys are not telling anyone where they have arrived from, or when, so far. They are very aware, apparently, that they would only be considered fools if they spoke the truth," Malic explained.

"Good. Not that they have any way of proving their story, but better that it isn't even discussed."

"They have the map, Damon. They could show someone else what they have discovered. Have you forgotten the map?" Malic asked.

"No, I have not forgotten the map, but I do not think they will use it to demonstrate with. If they become truly determined to get back to their time, they will not want to jeopardize their possession of the map by letting others know of it. I believe they will keep that a secret, but only until they do get back—if they figure out how to do that. *That* is when I will become concerned about the map."

"It is probably as you say, Damon. They will probably work alone until they get back—and—as you said, if they get back."

"Come Malic. A game of chess?"

"Yes, a game of chess—And this time…"

"Yes, I know—And this time you will defeat me…"

Damon smiled and placed his hand on Malic's shoulder, turning him toward the Falls of Learning.

"I see you are still remaining dry, my dear Malic."

Malic smiled, and walked into the waterfall emerging dry.

"Yes—dry as a mouthful of early persimmons."

"What an interesting analogy," Damon responded.

"Have you ever made that mistake?" Malic asked.

"No, I can't say that I have."

"Then you have no idea," Malic said, smiling.

CHAPTER 8

The Reality

Nightfall had arrived by the time Red and Jim reached Clermont's business district. Still dumbfounded by the story the oriental occupant of Laura's home had told them, they nearly walked right past the Hummingbird Café.

To their relief, it *was* still there. At least something familiar had survived their journey into the Lair! The door was open to the street, which seemed unusual in the chilly night air, but hunger called them through it without question. It wasn't until they passed through the opening that they noticed there was no door, but a warm upward flow of air separating the inside of the diner from the chilly outdoor air. Jim looked at Red and shrugged his shoulders, Red returning the gesture.

Although the name, Hummingbird Café, had survived, nothing else familiar about the diner had. The whole of the interior was glistening white and totally unfamiliar to the boys. The interior was bathed in light, but there was absolutely no source of the light visible to them. It was just there, emanating from everywhere, and yet, nowhere in particular.

There was still a counter, but *only* a counter, which made a U-turn at the end walls and followed the front windows where the booths had once been, stopping on either side of the front doorway. There were no stools, yet the customers *were sitting* at the counter, as if suspended from strings from the ceiling above. But, there were no strings.

Jim was the first to approach the counter, and trying to be as inconspicuous as he could under the circumstances, placed his hands on the counter and lowered himself slowly into a sitting position. His seat came to rest on something, yet nothing at all, suspended on, or supported by, something unseen, yet perfectly soft and comfortable. He smiled, turning back to look at Red.

Red approached the counter and took a "seat" next to Jim, totally amazed at not falling to the floor as he did so.

"This is weird," he offered.

"Too weird," Jim replied, smiling all the while.

"Where the hell are we?" Red asked his buddy.

"The Hummingbird Café, á la 2086," he answered, smiling an even larger smile.

"And—That doesn't freak you out a little?" Red asked him.

"Yeah, a little, but it's kinda cool, too. Don't you think so?" Jim asked.

"I guess, but it creates more problems than anything else," Red replied.

"Well, let's eat first and solve the problems later," Jim said. "I'm famished!"

"You're acting awfully cool about all this, Jim," Red observed.

"Red—That's because I'm scared shitless and don't know what to do about it! But, we've got to eat, so let's eat and figure everything else out later."

Jim looked over to where a rather elderly waitress was standing behind the counter. She didn't appear to be busy, so Jim called to her.

"Excuse me. Could we have a couple of menus, please?"

"The touch cube's right in front of you," she replied.

Touch cube? Jim thought. He looked and saw a small, transparent cube on the far edge of the counter. Reaching out toward it, he lightly placed his index finger on its top surface. Nothing happened. He retracted his finger slightly and tried touching the facing surface. To his amazement, a light began to glow from within the cube and as he looked up, there, in front of his face, suspended in the air, a menu. He reached out to touch it, but his hand went straight through it with no sensation of touch at all. It seemed to be projected there in mid air by the small cube on the counter surface.

"Wow, now that's awesome," he said to Red.

"I'll say," came Red's whispered reply.

"If they've got stuff like this out here in this little burgh, imagine what they must have in the big cities!" Jim marveled. "I mean, just imagine!"

"It's cool," Red said. "But look at what's on it, or rather, what's *not* on it. Where's the burgers and fries, or the steak and potatoes?"

"I see what you mean. What the hell is a colloidal dinner beverage?" Jim asked. "It sounds awful!"

"It sounds worse than that," Red replied, frowning at the thought.

"There's something that looks edible," Red pointed out. "Broiled faux beef, whatever that is. At least it says beef," he added, laughing.

"Faux means fake, Red. There's no telling what it really is, but we've got to eat, so let's give it a try—I guess."

Once again Jim tried to call the waitress over.

"We're ready to order," he called to her.

She walked over to the boys and leaned forward.

"Where are you boys from, anyway? Just touch the right side of the cube to solidify your menu and then touch the items you want. I'll get your order in that fashion," she whispered to them, sarcastically. "Where *are* you from?"

Jim took offense to her sarcasm and fired back.

"So, if that's all we have to do, what do they need you for?" he asked, just as spitefully as she had been sarcastic.

"I—bring you your food…You—tip me…"

She smiled a devilish smile their way and started to turn. Jim glanced down at her nametag, which read, "Laura". At first it didn't register, but a very brief moment later, it hit him. The waitress had stepped away and Jim called her back again.

"What now?" she asked, again with plenty of sarcasm.

"After we touch the items we want, how do we get rid of the menu in front of us?" he asked.

"When you are finished selecting your items, you touch the left side of the cube and it sends your order to the kitchen and closes the menu. Venus?"

"What?" Jim asked.

"Venus. That's where you're from, isn't it. Venus…"

"Cute, Laura. And—speaking of your name, are you any relation to Laura Palmer?" Jim sprung on her.

"You knew my aunt?" she asked, surprised at the question.

"Ah—No. We've just heard of her. From the lady who lives in her old house up the way," Jim answered, not knowing what else to say.

"Great. Listen, I don't want to hear any of your bullshit about her being crazy and all. Got it!" she barked in Jim's face. "My aunt had a hard life. She lost someone very dear to her up on Father Mountain and it drove her mad. She couldn't help herself. Keeping all those cats was just her way of coping with her loss, nothing more."

"Okay, okay," Jim interjected. "We didn't mean to get you upset, and we weren't going to make fun of her. We're—ah—folklore buffs, that's all. We search out folklore and legends during our vacation time from work in Illinois. We had a flat tire out in front of that oriental lady's house and pulled into her drive to see if she had a jack. We got to talking and the story of your aunt came out during our conversation."

"Flat tire? Jack? How the hell old is your car anyway?" Laura asked, with a very odd look on her face.

"Oh—it's a classic…Pretty old…A Jeep, to be exact…"

"Huh, my aunt had a Jeep once. Two of them as a matter of fact. How the hell did you drive that Jeep all the way out here?" she asked.

"What do you mean, how?" Red asked.

"If I remember correctly they all ran on gasoline. Where the hell did you get gasoline along the way?"

"Oh, that. We had it converted," Jim answered.

"To which?" Laura asked.

"The cheapest, what else?" Red responded, laughing as he tried to divert the answer to the question back to her.

"Carboline. Good choice. It fragments better in cold weather," Laura offered, much to the boys' relief.

"You guessed it," Red replied. "And that's exactly why we chose it, coming up here and all—and—it's cheaper."

"Thanks for your help with this touch cube thing. We don't have them on Venus," Jim quipped.

Laura smiled and winked at Jim and went back to her duties, which the boys weren't sure existed, unless they were all accomplished telepathically and conveyed to some machinery in the back room. She didn't seem to do anything at all until an order was ready. Then she actually did something. She took the dishes from an opening in the back wall and set them down on the counter in front of her. Then, they actually traveled along the counter right to the person they were intended for. The counter didn't move, just the dishes placed upon them, and they somehow found their way to the proper person. *Maybe,* Jim thought, *she is using a foot control,* but he doubted it after everything else he had seen of this place.

The boys placed their order, not knowing what they were actually ordering, and ate like they hadn't eaten in a week, which was nearly true. Despite the mystery of *what* they were eating, it *was* good. They finished every bite and then it hit Red like someone had dropped a brick square on his head.

"Jim," he whispered.

"What?"

"It just hit me. How the hell are we going to pay for this meal?" he asked.

"What do you…? Oh, yeah. Shit! All our money is ancient. Hell, we don't even know if they still use money!"

"Hey, Laura," Jim called to her.

Laura sauntered over to them.

"We're finished," he informed her, hoping she would volunteer their next step.

"Good. Just touch the back side of the cube and when the screen appears, enter your UAC," she explained.

"UAC?" Red asked, with a blank stare.

"Your Universal Account Code. Gad, you guys *are* from Venus!" she laughed.

"What if we don't have UAC's on Venus?" Jim asked, smiling his sweetest smile.

"What's up with you guys? Are you on the run from the law or something? Because, Venusians, if you are, by now the law already knows you are here," she informed them.

"We're not on the run," Red replied. "But, out of curiosity, how would they know we are here?" he asked.

Laura pointed up to the security camera behind the counter.

"FRS—Facial Recognition System. That camera is linked live into the NLECS, the National Law Enforcement Computer System," she explained, walking away to pick up an order.

"Nice," Jim replied. "That's pretty sharp!"

Red gave Jim a sideways kick to his calf and leaned toward him. He whispered, "Don't be so damn enthusiastic, okay? We're not supposed to be from 2002, so don't act like we are," he cautioned.

"Sorry, but this is cool! This whole future thing is cool!"

"Not to me! The way I see it, we screwed up Laura's life with our stupid search for that Lair. We are responsible for her going crazy. We ruined her life!" Red reminded his friend. "She spent the remainder of her life trying to figure out which bobcat was me. I guess she got it in her head that to go in there was to return a bobcat. I don't know, but that's the way it appears to me," Red finished.

"Sorry, buddy. You're right, of course. It's just that this is so surreal to me. I can't help but marvel at it."

"Well, instead of marveling at it, try figuring out a way to make right of it. Okay?" Red scolded. "There has to be something we can do to rectify our screw-up."

Laura returned momentarily with an offer for the boys.

"Look. It's obvious that you guys can't pay for your meal. So, I'll pick up your tab for you. You come round to my house tonight at eight thirty and I'll let you work it off around my place. I have a lot of work that needs to be done. Okay?"

"Sure," Red responded.

"Sounds good to me," Jim said.

"Fine. I live two doors down from my aunt's old house, toward town. Be there, okay? Now get the hell out of here before I change my mind."

Red scrambled out the doorway first, followed by Jim. Once out on the sidewalk, Jim noticed that the town was brightly lit in the dark of the evening. What's more, it was just like it had been in the diner. There was no apparent source of the light. It was just there, everywhere. He looked up through the light at the black sky and let out a "Whoop!" laughing and spinning in a swirl like a whirlwind.

"Jimbo! Get hold of yourself," Red warned. "You're going to call attention to us. We don't need *that*! Settle down! You're enjoying this, much too much!"

"I know, but it is awesome!" Jim exclaimed.

"Well don't get too used to it because we can't stay," Red insisted.

"Ha! We may have to, buddy. We may have to," Jim laughed.

Red knew that Jim may be right, but he was determined to get Laura's life back for her, if he could. He and Jim had stolen it as sure as they had come to Clermont. Their meddling with the future, or the past, or whatever had caused Laura to live a life of ridicule and torment was exclusively their fault. If there were any way to fix this, he was determined to find it.

"Jim, what do you think about going back into the Lair? Do you think there would be a way to reverse what we have done to Laura?" Red asked, obviously troubled.

"Red. I have no idea. If we go back in there we may come back out in the year 3000! Who knows? It would be a gamble at best," Jim replied, trying to help Red with his dilemma. He knew Red was taking the information about Laura's life after the Lair extremely hard.

"Maybe we could give it a test. Maybe go in, turn around and come out immediately. I mean five seconds in would be about five minutes out, right? That should relate to about seventy-one days out here. I did the math earlier; it's correct if everything remains constant. What remains to be seen is whether we go seventy-one days further into the future or back seventy-one days?"

"You've been giving this a lot of thought, Red. I'm impressed, but still, it's just speculation on your part that *anything* will remain constant."

"Well, I think that is what double curvilineal means. It means that the time spent going into the Lair is not the amount of time it will take to leave. At the same time, the time it takes to leave is relative to, but not equal to the time going on outside the Lair. Does that make sense to you?"

"Go on. Continue. Think it through out loud for me. I'll try to help solve it if I can," Jim offered.

"Okay. I believe all the times are relative. Our trip in was thirty minutes. Our trip out was thirty-six hours, but we slept six of those hours. So, the trip out would actually have taken thirty hours, or sixty times longer than the trip in. Okay, so if we travel into the Lair for only five seconds, our return trip should take five minutes. Got it?" Red asked.

"Yeah, I'm with you so far. Go on," Jim encouraged.

"Okay, that means we will be in the Lair exactly five minutes and five seconds. Now, originally, we were in there thirty-six and a half hours, approximately, and out here eighty-four and a quarter years passed by. Apply that ratio to our test trip and you find that seventy-one days will pass out here. Simple."

"Wow. I didn't know you could crunch numbers like that!"

"What the hell do you think I do at the foundry all day, sleep?" Red kidded.

"Okay," Jim began. "Seventy-one days will go by. Which way? To the future or to the past? That's the next problem," Jim finished.

"*That is* the next problem," Red agreed. "After we work off our meal at Laura's, we'll get a good night's rest and go back up there and find out the answer to that."

The boys did as they promised and arrived at Laura's on time, ready to do as she bid them do. They had taken a walking tour of the town to kill time before starting out the highway to her house, and they had found Clermont to be quite the changed place, to say the least.

To start with, the one traffic light in town had been removed. They had asked a passerby about it and they had been told that traffic lights had been unnecessary ever since 2080. The gentleman they talked with had acted like they were crazy to be asking and the boys had told him that they had been out of the country, studying in Europe, and hadn't received an explanation for the lack of traffic lights in the U.S. yet. That seemed to satisfy his curiosity as to their ignorance of the situation and he had gone on to explain it to them.

They learned that three super computers linked with a network of satellites now controlled the signal lights, which were now located in the vehicles themselves. The lights were an invisible part of the windshield, which glowed red, yellow or green upon approaching a designated intersection. Somehow, the three super computers kept it all straight throughout the entire country. What's more, if you violated a signal zone while you were in the "red zone", your car's onboard computer would print you out a violation receipt as it transmitted the information to the Central Traffic Administration. As if that hadn't been enough of a shock to the boys, they then learned that the driver's universal account was then debited the penalty amount for the violation, automatically, and instantly. He had gone on to explain that speeding violations were handled in the same manner.

"The whole country is grid worked with speed limit information transmitters," he explained. "The satellites monitor this and the vehicles passing through the various speed zones. Go too fast, and out of your dashboard pops a ticket! Out of your universal account goes your money!"

"That's crazy!" Jim exclaimed. "That's 'Big Brother' for sure!"

"Yes, but it's not all bad," he offered. "At least no one can steal your vehicle unless they physically tow it away."

"Why's that?" Jim asked, interested in an explanation for this 'future' development.

"When you buy a car you get a ring that you wear on your finger. If the ring isn't within three or so feet of the ignition module, the vehicle won't start and there is no way to hotwire it either. There are no wires in the ignition systems, only chips and transmitters to do the job. Without the ring, the onboard computer is disabled."

"Well, at least that's a good thing," Jim commented.

"Yes, it is, and the ring is also how the super computers know who is driving a vehicle and know who to charge for a violation," he explained further.

"What if you want to borrow someone's car?" Red asked.

"Then you borrow the owner's ring and he takes the chance of getting a violation for your misdeed. It makes people think twice about who they lend their vehicle to."

They never did get an explanation for where the well-lit streets obtained their light, but they did discover something even more fascinating when Red observed that the stars overhead looked normal, but the stars nearer the horizon seemed larger than normal. It was explained to them that it was the *biosphere effect.*

The gentleman they asked about the appearance of the stars wasn't up on all the technicalities of the phenomena, but knew that scientists had developed a way to generate a dome over populated cities using the molecules present in the air itself.

"Just turn on the 'current' and the invisible dome forms above the specified area coming to within two feet of the ground," he began. "Somehow they have made it economical enough so that there is an energy savings involved in the process. Even a small place like Clermont can afford the system. The dome traps available heat, creating less use of furnaces in homes and businesses, and the reverse is true of air conditioning in hot weather. In addition to those benefits, the dome also filters out about fifty percent of the harmful ultraviolet rays from the Sun, greatly reducing cataracts and skin cancers among the population, but still allowing plant life beneath its protective shield."

"Excuse me," Jim interrupted. "But, I didn't notice any dome when we came into town. You said it comes to within two feet of the ground, right?"

"Yes. That's the true beauty of the technology. The dome is not actually solid, but permeable enough for planes to fly through, cars to drive through and people to walk through. You don't even notice it's there. It keeps the rain out under normal power, but the 'juice' can be reduced to allow even rain to penetrate."

"That's too cool," Jim said, when the gentleman had finished.

Even Red, with his preoccupation on Laura, was impressed, but not enough for any further explanations.

"Yeah, that's really neat. Thanks for the explanation, sir. Jim—Come on. Let's get going to Laura's place," he said, in a commanding voice.

The boys left town heading down the highway to Laura's. Jim, of course, had to keep stopping as they neared the edge of Clermont to try to find the exact spot where the dome came down to the ground. He found that the gentleman in town had been right. He could not locate it.

"We must have already walked right through it," he said to Red, after they were a good distance from the business district.

Red just smiled. They were getting closer to Laura's now and that felt like the first step toward getting back to "Aunt Laura". "Aunt Laura". That thought alone was enough to send a chill up his spine. *How the hell could this happen?* he thought, as they turned into Laura's drive.

Laura greeted them warmly upon their arrival and put them to work pulling up carpet, scraping paint, painting and paper hanging. None of this had changed by 2086. Remodeling was still remodeling. Laura told them that a lot of innovations in home decorating had fallen by the wayside because women still preferred the old way of doing things. "They still like going to the paint store and picking out colors and they still insist on looking through real wallpaper books," she explained.

Laura had a full-blown renovation project going on in her house and the boys were the answer to her prayers. They worked until midnight; doing whatever project she had lined up next. At midnight, she offered them a snack and a place to sleep. She explained that she had to get up in the morning and go back to the diner, so midnight was her usual quitting time on her renovation projects.

Jim, however, saw an opportunity to help themselves as well as Laura, and negotiated a deal with her. They would stay the day tomorrow and continue working on her house if the next day she would drive them up to the end of Access Road 27 and drop them off there. Jim explained to her that he had heard somewhere about a successful rancher named Carter Elliott who had purchased Father Mountain some years ago and never put it to any good use. He went on to explain that ever since he had heard about it, he had wanted to go there and have a look around.

"Don't ask me why," he told her. "It's just one of those things that gets in your craw and you can't leave it alone. I just want to have a look around up there. I also heard that there is a cool lake and waterfall there that might be worth checking out."

Laura's response to Jim's explanation was cold. First she pointed out that Carter Elliott had not been thought well of around Clermont and had passed away around 2050, much to the approval of the locals. Then she continued, saying, "I wouldn't know about Father Mountain or any lake or waterfall. I've never been up there. I do know that my aunt's troubles all began up there, so I'd be careful if I were you. In fact, if I *were* you, I wouldn't go up there at all," she added. "But you do as you will. I'll drop you up there day after tomorrow if you do a good job here for me tomorrow."

That settled she showed the boys to where they could bed down for the night.

"By the way," she said, as she was turning to leave the room. "I don't even know your names."

Jim started to answer, but Red cut him off before he could get out a single word.

"I'm Carl," he lied, "and this is Ted," he said, pointing to Jim.

"Well, Carl and Ted. It's good to have you here. Sleep well. I haven't had visitors since Aunt Laura passed away."

"By the way," Red said to her. "Was it your dad or your mother that was your Aunt Laura's sibling?"

"My dad was her younger brother. Why do you ask?"

"Just curious. When you mention her it sounds as if you were quite fond of her," Red answered. "I was just wondering what happened to her to make her…ah, well, to make her…"

"Crazy?" Laura filled in what Red was having trouble getting out. "No one really knows for sure. She went up on Father Mountain one day in July of 2002. She came back ranting and raving about some boy named Red who had vanished up there. Vanished into some sort of hole in the air, or so she said. Somehow, she got to believing that this Red fellow had turned into a bobcat and she started collecting bobcats for the rest of her life. Looking for the right one, I suppose, but who really knows. What I do know is that she was a sweet lady who was always kind to me—growing up—and that's enough for me."

"So, who was Red?" Red asked.

"No one knows. He may never have existed at all for all anyone knows. There's no telling where she got that name, or the notion that he had become a bobcat."

"Thanks for the explanation, Laura. That's an interesting story," Red commented. "Did your Aunt Laura ever marry?" he asked.

"Nope. Never did. I guess she went to her grave still looking for Red—but a bobcat? That's what always baffled me. Still does. What did she think she was going to do, marry a bobcat? Maybe she thought she could turn him back into a man or something. Who knows?"

"Maybe," Red whispered. "Maybe she did. Anyway, thanks for the story, Laura."

"Sure, boys. Get a good night's sleep," she said, as she closed the door behind her.

Red turned to Jim who had been listening intently to the tale.

"Boy, that's sad. Look what we did to her. We've got to fix this mess, somehow."

"We'll try, day after tomorrow. Let's get some shut-eye for now though," Jim told Red.

"Yeah, good idea. I'm bushed."

The boys' second night's sleep in 2086 was sound. Red awoke to the sound of the back door closing as Laura departed for the diner. He rolled over and glanced at the clock on the dresser. *Eight o'clock—man did I sleep good,* he thought, as he rose up from his pillow and stood beside the bed. Jim was still out like a light on the pallet Laura had constructed for him yesterday. Red pulled on his jeans and then carefully stepping over Jim, headed for the kitchen.

He was comforted by the fact that the kitchen was *not* the modern marvel that the diner had been. It was as conventional as he knew kitchens to be in 2002. He pulled a chair out from under the table and sat down to read the note Laura had left folded on the tabletop. It was a list of instructions for their day's activities and finished by offering them anything they wanted to eat and drink throughout the day.

Red placed the note back on the tabletop and leaning back in the chair, stretched and yawned. *2086*, he thought. *Never in a million years would I have believed this two days ago!* He pushed his chair back from the table and standing, walked to the refrigerator. Nothing looked familiar in there, but then why would it? *Eighty-four years changes a lot*, he reasoned, and began reading labels. After a few minutes study he had located ersatz bacon and some sort of egg substitute. He looked over at the range and thought to himself, *Now, if I can figure out how to work that I'll be in good shape!*

"Good morning, Red," Jim said, wandering shakily into the kitchen.

"Hey, Jim. Good morning," Red greeted him. "You're just in time to help me figure this stove out. I found 'bacon and eggs' in the fridge, but I haven't figured the stove out yet."

"Well it can't be too hard," Jim commented. "Let me give it a try."

Between the two boys and five minutes of experimenting with the controls, they had heat on the left-rear burner pad.

"See, I told you we could figure it out," Jim said, smiling. "You doing the cooking?" he asked.

"Yep. I'll cook and you look over Laura's set of instructions for our day. Figure out what we should do first while I get breakfast ready. And—also—see if you can find any salt and pepper."

Jim located the salt and pepper and studied the note, planning out the work sequence for the day. Red finally figured out how to get breakfast right on his second attempt, wasting a few strips of "bacon" and about a cup of "egg" stuff. When they finally were able to eat Red's efforts, they found the substitute breakfast items to be quite palatable. Their impression of the breakfast of the future was favorable, but not as welcomed as the real thing would have been. Still, it was food and it was tasty. Their hunger staved and the dishes rinsed, they went to work on Laura's home improvement list.

The work proceeded well and they accomplished a lot before Laura's return at eight p.m. She was not only impressed with their work, but in fact, delighted with how much they had accomplished. The boys had completely finished the dining room and front hall and were nearly half done with the master bedroom.

"Wow, you did great today! Is there any way I can convince you two to stay a few more days?" she asked.

"We'd love to, Laura, but unfortunately we have to get back to our own lives, as mundane as they are. Sorry," Red replied.

"I didn't think so. It was too much to hope for, I guess. Anyway—You two clean up and I'll cook you a big supper. How's that sound to you?" she asked.

Red and Jim expressed their unanimous approval for her offer and departed for the bathroom to wash up.

"You know, Red. We could stay and help her out a bit. What's the harm in that?" Jim asked.

"The problem with that is that we are missing from the year 2002, that's what," he replied. "And—we have to get back there and fix this mess!"

"You don't know that we are missing from 2002. We may still be there, going about life as usual. Just because we somehow ended up in 2086, doesn't mean we actually left 2002, does it?" Jim asked.

Red stared at Jim blankly, and then answered, "You know—I don't know. Is that possible?" he replied, questioning the realities of their situation.

"Is it possible that we are even here?" Jim asked. "If you accept the notion that we actually *jumped* to the year 2086, then you have to entertain the notion that it may be possible for us to still be back in

2002. I mean—once you realize that traveling to the future is possible, then you have to throw away the rule book of life as we know it to be, or thought it to be."

"I suppose you could be right about that. Who the hell knows? It's all too unbelievable in the first place. Wait, though. Laura said Laura spent her whole life looking for me after that day in Lynx Canyon. We *must* have actually left 2002 completely. We must still be missing from there."

"Red. You're thinking conventionally. Think outside the box. This is 2086. The year 2002 is in the past. At this point in time, we never came back to 2002. It's over with, and we are dead and gone, forgotten, unless you had planned on living to be over a hundred years old back then. My point is—that we are not missing from 2002. That's in the past and over with. Somehow, we are in the here and now and *that* is the year 2086. How long we hang around here makes no difference to anybody but the people we come in contact with here and now."

"And—to us," Red reminded Jim.

"Yes, and to us," Jim conceded.

"Look, Jim. Right now my only concern is to try to figure out a way to rectify the mess we made of Laura's life. That's all. I want to fix things for her. I know I keep harping on that, but that is the way I feel. We messed her up. We have to try to undo that mess."

"You want to *be* with her, you mean. You think that if you can get back and fix things you can be with her again, right?" Jim pointed out, bluntly.

"Okay. Yes, I want to be with her again. What's wrong with that?" Red asked.

"Nothing, but is it possible? We don't know. Can we *get* back? Again, we don't know. So what's the hurry? Why not explore this new world and see what it has to offer?"

"Because, Jim, the longer we stay here the more likely that we'll be found out," Red answered.

"No. The idea of us being from another time is so foreign to anyone's thinking that no matter how backward we seem to these people, *that* idea will never be a consideration to them. It won't cross their minds, not in a million years," Jim explained.

"You don't know *that* for sure. Maybe *time-travel* is something these people have discovered by now," Red speculated.

"Nope. It's not. If that were true, they'd have visited us back in 2002. We weren't visited, indicating to me that general time-travel, as a matter of everyday existence *never* was discovered at *any* time in the future. *We* now know it's possible, but it certainly isn't, wasn't, or will it ever be a common thing in any period of time."

"Boys!" Laura's voice came from the kitchen. "You get lost?"

"We'll finish this later," Red said. "But, we're not hanging around here any longer than we have to. We're going to the Lair tomorrow, like we planned, and we are going to test our theory about the time ratios. That's what we are going to do. Nothing else."

Laura's supper was a delight. Neither Red, nor Jim was quite sure they knew *what* they were eating, but whatever the menu items were, they were good and very satisfying. Dessert, again a mystery, was delicious. Laura called it liola cake and whatever else liola might be it was tasty.

After supper the boys finished up the work they had been doing in the master bedroom and decided to retire early, at ten thirty. As they said goodnight, Laura told them that they would leave at seven thirty in the morning and she would drop them at the end of 27. She also offered to pick them up on 27 after she finished work at seven thirty in the evening, but the boys declined that offer explaining they didn't know how long they would want to stay up there.

"Well, when you get done up there, come on back and I'll have your beds waiting and a hot meal on the stove," she told them.

At ten a.m. the following morning, Red tossed a rock into the Lair.

"It's still there," he said to Jim.

CHAPTER 9

The Test of Time

The rock had vanished. Red and Jim sat side by side on the ground, looking into the void that was the Cats' Lair. It was as invisible as it had been before, nothing outwardly indicating its presence, yet the boys knew all too well that it was there.

"Even if your logic is right, Red, how are we going to know which way we went after we come out, *if* we come out?" Jim asked.

"The weather?" Red suggested, questioning that idea even as he spoke it. "If I'm right, we'll be back in roughly a little over two months. If we go forward it will be December and a lot colder. If we go back, it will be August and a lot hotter. That's how we'll know," Red offered.

"That's not good enough," Jim replied. "We might go two years and two months forward and it will still be December and cold, but we'll be off by two years. Furthermore, we might go *back* ten months and it will also be December and cold. That's not good enough."

"Okay, then—What do you suggest?" Red asked, rubbing his chin in thought.

"We take your hunting knife and we strip the bark from an area of that pine tree over there. If we come back and there is no bark missing and the surface is unscarred, then we will know we went back to before we damaged it. That won't tell us how far we went back, but we'll know we went back. But—if we go forward the bark will be damaged still, and we can get an idea from the amount of regeneration that has taken place as to approximately how long we were gone. Two months alone will not give it time to repair itself much at all, but several years will produce a good amount of repair, yet allow us to see that it was once damaged where we stripped it."

"Good idea! Now that's thinking. Let's get started!" Red praised Jim, with enthusiasm. "Here," he said, handing Jim the knife, "You do the honors."

Jim took the knife and carefully stripped a one-foot long by six-inch wide section of bark from the tree. Then he thought of something else, and drove the knife as deeply as he could into the tree's trunk.

"We'll leave the knife there to see how much rusting occurs while we're away. That'll be another indicator," he explained.

"What happens to the knife if we go backwards in time?" Red asked.

"What do you mean?" Jim questioned Red, cocking his head and raising his brow.

"If we go back the knife won't be here when we return. Where will it be then?" he asked Jim. "Back in its sheath on my side—or someplace else?"

"Hell if I know. Two months ago, out here, we were in the Lair and so was your knife."

"But the knife isn't going back into the Lair. It's staying here, so it can't travel back with us. It also can't be in the tree before we put it there so if we go back it will not be in the tree when we emerge. Where will it be?" Red asked, again.

"I have no idea where it would be," Jim admitted. Maybe it ceases to exist until two months pass and then it reappears in the tree at the time we originally put it there. That must be it. It's in limbo until then…Understand?"

"No I don't, any more than you do, but it's an explanation we can live with," Red laughed. "Ready?"

"Ready."

Red took the lead, getting down on his hands and knees. Jim got down and took his position directly behind him. They crawled into the Lair, Red counting aloud, "One Mississippi—Two Mississippi—Three Mississippi—Four Mississippi—Five Mississippi—TURN!"

They turned and began crawling outward down the tunnel as Jim noted the time on his watch. Four minutes later they were still crawling. Four and a half minutes later Jim could still see only white. Five minutes later his head plowed into something cold and wet.

"What the hell!" he shouted.

"What's wrong?" Red asked, momentarily panic-stricken.

"Snow!" Jim yelled back to Red.

"Well keep going! Every second we are in here is days out there!" he urged.

Jim started digging upward and away from the Lair, Red following as close to his backsides as he could. Jim's head finally broke the surface of the five-foot blanket of snow that had fallen at some point while they were in transit.

"Damn! How much time did we waste?" Red asked as he popped out onto the surface of the snow.

"Only a minute or so," Jim replied.

"Shit, that's about two weeks!" Red informed him.

"So, what difference does two weeks make. So it may be January instead of December, so what? It sure as hell isn't August!" he pointed out, needlessly.

"Yeah, you're right. It doesn't make any difference. Let's check the tree and the knife."

They went straight to the tree, realizing immediately that they were going to have to get back into the Lair, and soon. They were quickly growing extremely uncomfortable in the freezing cold, something they had not prepared themselves for. Jim's best guess was that it was close to zero and they were in shirtsleeves.

"Damn," Red said, brushing away snow, which had collected on the trunk of their tree. "The bark is missing!"

"We went forward then. And, it's hardly any different than when we left it. I'd say your timing is on the money big fella," Jim stated, smiling, but with reserve.

"Check the knife," Red said.

Jim removed the knife, cleaning snow from the blade, and said, "Pretty damn clean. Hardly any rust at all. Again, it looks like your timing is dead nuts, Red."

"Shit! How the hell do we go back then?" he asked Jim, wrinkling his brow, obviously very distressed over this development. "How in the hell do we get back? We've got to get back into the Lair and get out of this cold, travel another six months into warmer weather. About twelve seconds this time."

"That will take us further into the future, Red."

"I know, but we'll just have to worry about that then. We'll freeze to death if we stay here now!" he advised.

"Okay then, let's get going," Jim stated, turning quickly for the tunnel he had dug through the snow. "I'll go in first, you follow."

As Red emerged from the Lair, he was bathed in warmth. Much to his relief, it felt like summer, but it was the dead of night. It seemed as though his theory on the relative times involved in the Lair were bearing out. *That* was about all he was happy about.

"It's night time!" he exclaimed. "I didn't expect that. Funny, but I never even gave the thought of coming out at night any consideration. At least it's warm though," he stated, happily. "That should have been about six more months, Jim. Check the tree and the knife if you can see them well enough. See if they look consistent with our timing," Red instructed.

Jim did as Red asked and although dark, he was able to determine that the scarring on the tree was still relatively fresh and the knife, although a little more rusty, was not flaking or anything like that. He decided that, more than likely, only the eight months they had hoped for had passed by while they were in the Lair. This was the good news. The bad news was that they were no closer to a solution for going back in time than they were at the beginning of their experiment.

The weary *travelers* sat down on the soft, pine needle strewn ground, and in silence began thinking about what to do next. By now, Laura would have no idea what had happened to them after she had dropped them off at the end of Access Road 27. Had another search taken place in their absence? Had they now created two *victims* of their time travels? There were a lot of questions that needed answers and *one* solution needed to be found.

They could go back to Laura's house and "reappear" there. It was only eight months later, though it would require a pretty wild explanation of where they had vanished to, and why. If they couldn't figure out a way to go back in time, fitting into this time appeared to be the only solution to their current dilemma. At least with a contact like Laura, they had a way to casually merge into 2087, which is when it was now by Red's reckoning.

The problem in that, which may have already arisen, was that Laura was old, probably sixty-five as they had it figured. What if she had passed on while they were in transit to now? They could only hope that that had not happened. Making the hike back to Laura's seemed the next logical step…after coming up with a cover story as to where they had been the past eight months.

"Hey, Red."

"What?" Red asked.

"What if that tunnel goes only one way?" Jim asked, seriously considering the possibility.

"Don't even…" Red paused and rubbed his chin. "…think it," he finished.

"Well, the Indian came from 1800 something to 1998. Did he ever actually get back? We don't know. He disappeared, true enough, but to where? Gillespie said that the farmer went from 1930 to 1990—forward, again, but what happened to him?" Jim asked.

"You seem to think that he might be the same Carter Elliott that bought the ranch out here. When did Laura say he died?"

"I think she said it was around 2050, if I remember correctly, why?"

Red explained that if Carter Elliott was the same man who had owned the farm and the ranch, he had lived about one hundred and fifty years.

"Think about it. Gillespie said he looked about thirty, *both* times he saw him. Okay, that puts his birth at around 1900. He should have been ninety when Gillespie saw him the second time, and—he would have been one hundred and fifty by the time he died around 2050! How can you explain that except for the fact that he gained sixty years in the Lair?" Red asked.

"Or, Gillespie is all wet," Jim said, conceding the possibility.

"That's what I may have thought before, but not necessarily so now. Not after what we have experienced. I think Gillespie saw exactly what he said he saw and was correct in his observation," Red surmised.

"So he never went back in time, just forward?" Jim asked.

"Sure. Now that I think about it, your premise from before that he went back to Illinois to settle his business and burry the map was all wrong. He couldn't have gone back sixty years later to settle his business. His relatives or the state would have settled it long ago, when he went missing in 1930. If he had used the Lair to go back to 1930 to settle his business and bury the map, he'd still be thirty in 1930 with no way to gain access to the Lair again. Remember, without the map you can't locate or use the Lair. So, now he's thirty years old in 1930...again. No way he lives until 2050," Red explained to Jim.

"Then—ah—How did the map get buried back on his farm in Illinois?" Jim asked.

"I don't know why he went back, but I'll bet he went back after 1990, after coming out of the Lair. That's when he buried the map, on a trip back to his old home, maybe just to see it again. While there, he buried the map to prevent its ever being used again," Red theorized.

"So we have two *time travelers* that we know of who appear to have gone only forward in time? That's just great! Then how do we get back?" Jim complained.

"Maybe we don't," Red answered, in a solemn, whispering tone. "Maybe it does go only one way. Think about it. If it were a two way street then everyone who went forward could come back and tell about it. It would be a documented fact, even in our original time. They could bring something back from the future to prove their story, too."

"And—It won't work that way in reverse," Jim pointed out. "Anyone can have something from the past. That's proof of nothing. Then add the element of being able to change the future and you have a world of problems that would crop up. You can't change the future, based on what you find there if you can't get back to make the changes. I think this whole damned Lair place was based on that notion," Jim explained, shaking his head and sighing. "I think we are stuck right here, unless you want to go even further forward."

"But if a guy like Carter Elliott wanted to prove he had come from another time, he had Gillespie to bear out his story. Gillespie saw him. Gillespie knew because he did see him in two different time periods at the same age both times. That's proof, kinda anyway."

"Yeah, Red, but why would he want to go and shoot down his only hope of getting back home to his own time? If he could convince people that he had traveled from the past into their time, it would only be a matter of a very short time before the authorities would take control of the Lair. For any hope of returning to his own time he would have to insure that he retain control of the Lair. He would have to allow himself time to try to figure out how to use it to get home again. I think Carter Elliott did just that and finally came to the realization that it couldn't be done. That is when he went back to Illinois and buried the map."

"Jim—I sure hope you're wrong. I sure as hell don't want to stay here and I sure as shit don't want to go any further forward!"

"Then let's assume I'm wrong and try to figure out how to get back. It's worth a try and we sure as hell have nothing to lose for our efforts."

They sat there on the pine needles and studied the Lair until they were too tired to continue. They lay down and soon fell asleep, still trying to think of a solution to their entrapment in the future, which had become their present situation.

Morning found them no closer to a solution. There were no revelations in their dreams, or even helpful hints. As the dew began to dry from the surrounding forest floor, they were still inextricably implanted in 2087.

Red had awakened staring into the eyes of a large bobcat.

"Shit," he whispered. *Lie still*, he thought.

The bobcat studied his face intently. Red could hear it purring, which was encouraging, but not enough so to move even a muscle. He held his breath and closed his eyes, trying to play dead. *Maybe that will work*, he thought, against all hope. When he could hold it no longer he let out his breath as quietly as he could and opened his eyes. The cat was gone. He turned his head, quickly, in the direction of the Lair just in time to see the bobcat disappear into it.

"Jim!" he yelled. "Did you see that?"

"What?" Jim replied, through a yawn.

"That bobcat, that's what! It was right here staring into my face when I woke up!"

"You must have been dreaming. No bobcat is going to get that close to you," was Jim's only reply.

"Yeah. No ordinary bobcat maybe. But this one wasn't any ordinary bobcat."

"What the hell are you talking about, not ordinary?" Jim asked, disturbed at his rude awakening.

"This cat talked to me. I mean he communicated with me, not talked, actually. He gave me a message, somehow, in my head," Red tried to explain, but totally confused over the whole event and not able to collect his thoughts properly.

"Ha! Now I know you were dreaming. What did this talking bobcat have to say to you?" Jim asked, laughing loudly, barely able to get the words out through the ensuing gasps for breath.

"He said, *'You have been warned once. Go back to whence you came, dispose of your map, and be not found here again.'* Then…he had a message for you. He knew your name, too. He said, *'Tell James that his cousin never meant to break his finger. It was truly an accident.'* What the hell does that mean, Jim?"

Jim's eyes were fixed on Red's. They stared in disbelief into Red's with the look of a man who had just survived a near fatal event. They were wide and round and swimming.

"Jim? You okay?" Red asked his friend.

"Yeah—Okay."

"What's the message mean?" Red asked again.

"It means that he *did* communicate with you, but how?—I had a cousin named Lewis. We were wrestling one day in my back yard when I was about six years old. He was eleven. He broke my finger and I always believed that he had done it on purpose, that's all. I guess maybe not."

"What do we do about the other part of the message?" Red asked, unsure of even how he felt about it.

"I don't know. Let me think about it for a few minutes."

Jim lay down on his back looking up through the pine boughs at the brightening sky. He closed his eyes and thought about the message. Red lay back down, too, and thought about Laura, the young

Laura, not her niece, the old Laura, and a tear came to his eye. He thought about home—and more tears came.

It was about twenty minutes before Jim came to his conclusion. He rolled to his side and, reaching over, nudged Red.

"Hey, Red. I think this is bullshit. I think they, whoever *they* is, are trying to hide something. I think the warnings are designed to scare us away from the truth about this place. If they know about my cousin, Lewis, and if they can make bobcats do their bidding, then *they* are in control, not us. So why bother with a bunch of warnings? Why not just get rid of us if they don't want us here?"

"I don't know, Jim. Why don't they?" Red responded.

"Because they can't, that's why? For whatever reason, they can't override our free will to be here. They have nothing to say about it and there is nothing they can directly do about it. All they have at their disposal is the ability to *try* to scare us off. *That's* got to be the answer!" Jim stated, jubilantly. "Something tells me that they are powerless to directly forbid us to do what we will or to directly dispose of us. What do you think of that, Red?"

"I think you may be on to something there. But, *who are they?*" Red asked Jim, totally without a clue as to the answer to that question.

"I haven't the foggiest. Aliens? Demons? Ghosts? Ancient Indian medicine men? I don't know—yet—but I'm going to try my damnedest to find out," he stated, emphatically. "I want to go home, too, just like you, Red. I think this future world is neat and interesting, but I don't want to stay here forever. If there is something that they are hiding about how we can get back home, I'm going to do everything I can think of to figure it out."

Red liked the way Jim was talking now. He liked it a lot, and he was more than willing to help Jim solve their problem.

"So, where do we start?" he asked Jim.

"We start at the beginning, when I first set eyes on the map."

CHAPTER 10

The Other Side

"*D*amon. Has Glasic returned from his task?"

"Yes, Otheon, he has indeed returned, but with bad news, I fear."

"What bad news has he brought to us, Damon?"

"The boys who located Carter Elliott's map are stubborn. They seem to be ignoring our warnings. They are set on trying to figure out a way back to their time."

"Let them try if they will, we have fulfilled our obligation of providing them with the clue they need. It is in the Father's hands now."

"But, Otheon, they *are* persistent. They have been experimenting with the time ratios within the portal and they appear to have figured out two of the time ratios and how they work together in relationship with the outside world. They may prove to be worthy adversaries in the end if we allow them free reign in the portal."

"Very well, Damon, send Malic to them and we will see if *he* can *persuade* them to abandon their efforts and resolve to stay in their present time ring. But I fear, my dear Damon, that if they are as determined and worthy as you claim, it will be to no avail."

"I, too, Otheon. I fear these two boys have more resolve than the others who have ventured into the portal. I'm afraid they will upset the balance of things with their determination to find a way home. You know, Otheon, we can not allow *that* to happen."

Damon. *You* know—as well as I, that we are powerless to prevent it if they have that measure of resolve."

"Yes, Otheon, I realize that. If only Caspeic had not drawn that map and vested in it the powers of passage we would not find ourselves in this situation every few centuries that pass. That map jeopardizes all we are here working for."

"And Carter Elliott understood that and took the map a thousand miles away, burying it where he thought it would be safe. Who was to know this young James Preston would retrieve it and once again bring us to this point? If only there were a way to destroy the map."

"Yes, if only—or deprive them of the map all together."

"And again, Damon, you know *that* is not possible either. Free will *does* prevail over our desires, even if it is not in the best interest of the world and the Kinder."

"And tell me again why the portal can not be relocated and I shall scream a scream that will surely be heard in Heaven, dear Otheon.

"It *is* the Father's will that it remain where it is—now scream, Damon. I wish to hear your explanation when the Father hears it On High," Otheon laughed. "*That* I truly wish to hear."

"Never mind your wishes, Otheon. I'll arrange for Malic to *greet* the boys near the portal's entrance. Perhaps he can turn this about—one more time."

Damon spun about and left to prepare Malic, once again, to try to rectify the carelessness of Caspeic. As he walked down the passage leading to the portal tunnel he thought of poor old Caspeic and his inability to find his way home from his assignments. Far too many times one of the Guardians had to be sent to retrieve him home. Then, one day Caspeic had had his bright idea. He would draw a map and bless it with the powers of passage. The need for the blessing was a function of his terrible memory as well. When Caspeic did manage to find his way back to the portal's location, quite frequently he had forgotten the incantation that would open it to his entry.

Damon smiled. *Poor Caspeic*, he thought. *Why does the Father put up with you?* But Damon knew the answer. The Father's patience was legendary and he had long ago forgiven Caspeic for his thoughtless mistake. Not the mistake of creating the map, as the Father understood Caspeic's need for it, but losing it was different. *That* mistake jeopardized the secrecy of the portal and the secret of the Guardians themselves and might one day lead to disaster.

Damon stopped at that thought. *What would happen if mankind discovered that their time ran concurrent with all other times in perpetual circles of life? What would happen if they actually discovered that what they thought had happened years before was actually happening at that very moment they thought about it? There was always a first time something happened. That was the present. But, there was almost never a last time, not until the last human never thought of it again. That defined the past.* These were thoughts that Damon did not like to dwell on for long. The potential for abuse of this knowledge was frightening to him. He knew the Kinder to be extremely resourceful beings. If they understood what it was that time actually was, they would find a way to do exactly what the portal allows the Guardians to do; go to whatever point in time they desire. The portal was all that was needed to *jump* from one circle of life to any other concurrent circle. *And how would the Kinder handle that ability?* Damon shuddered at that thought.

Damon continued down the corridor to Malic's quarters. Upon knocking, Damon entered to find Malic, engaged in a game of chess with Oric.

"Hello, Malic," Damon greeted. "Oric, how are you today?"

Oric nodded and smiled as Malic rose from his chair.

"I know—it's the boys, correct?" Malic asked.

"Yes, Malic, it is the boys. They are a persistent lot and we need you to go and do what you can to dissuade them from continuing their quest."

"So it shall be done, Damon. I'll leave momentarily—it's my move," he said, smiling.

Damon left the two to come to a stopping point in their game and proceeded to Otheon's chambers. When he entered, Otheon was studying Red and Jim, sitting outside the portal. The fingers of each of his hands were at his temples as he studied his mental vision of the two boys discussing their next move.

"Sorry to disturb you, Otheon. Malic is preparing to leave now."

"Thank you, Damon. Perhaps, with any luck at all, we will be able to avoid disclosing ourselves once again. Malic, hopefully, will be able to persuade these boys to leave and adapt to life in their current time ring."

"I have my doubts this time," Damon said. "These boys are different. The Indian, Little Hawk, was superstitious and easily frightened off. Carter Elliott was an adult and prone to accepting what came his way and dealing with it in the framework of his current condition. But—these boys are just that—boys. Their adolescence drives them to explore the unknown and challenge authority. Malic may not be able to *persuade* them given the tools he is permitted to use."

"Pray that you are wrong, Damon. If their free will brings them to the solution they seek, we will be forced to confront them and divulge ourselves. Never in the history of *this* world has that been necessary. The ramifications are unknown—and could be catastrophic. The Kinder, as well you know, are a spirited lot. I do not wish to discover how they would deal with the knowledge we possess."

"Nor do I, dear Otheon, nor do I," Damon concurred.

"Otheon, you've been here since the beginning. Perhaps you can help *me* understand. I was a mere aide when this last occurred. First, why is it that the Father does not punish these human intruders?"

"They have broken no laws by coming here, Damon. The Father is just and would never punish one of his children if they have broken no laws. The portal is invisible to them, but for Caspeic's map. The Father never prohibited their entry because it was thought to be impossible for them to even learn of its existence. Therefore, no laws were written in regard to it. The mistake was Caspeic's, not that of the Kinder."

"I can understand the reasoning behind that, but why does the Father insist upon us providing a clue to the Kinder that might one day lead them to the secret of going *back* in time, jumping to a previous time ring? Just look at how much these two boys have figured out already. Why provide them with a clue to traveling back?"

"Again, Damon, the Father is compassionate and knows that once trapped in a future world the misguided human will be in despair. He simply wants to provide them with some hope of returning to their own ring. Those three words, *double reverse curvilineal*, provide the root of the hope. When told the portal is double reverse curvilineal they intuitively know that the answer to their returning home lies within the description we have provided to them. But, they have trespassed where they were not invited, so the Father insists that they be clever and figure out the answer for themselves. All He is doing in providing the clue is providing the hope of one day finding their way home."

"I see," Damon said, with a look of enlightenment on his face. "And what of the map? I have heard you say that it can not be taken from whomever possesses it, but why is that?" Damon questioned. "I have heard you mention free will when it is discussed, but how does free will come into play in regard to the map?"

"The Father has stated that the map must be relinquished of free will by whomever possesses it. Actually, He has stated that it must be volunteered of free will. We are not even free to ask for it, only suggest that whomever possesses it, destroy it if they can, or hide it away securely where it may not be used again."

"As Carter Elliott tried to do."

"And the boys," Otheon reminded Damon. "They tried to burn it in their campfire, but to no avail. Then they realized that it was their only hope of entering the portal again and possibly the key to their returning home."

"I guess the Father knows best," Damon said. "I think I'll go to where I can watch Malic do his work. Unlike you, Otheon, I can't see the portal from here. Unlike you, Otheon, my vision is still limited."

Damon retreated from Otheon's chambers and proceeded in the direction of his windowed chamber. It took at least a millennium to develop complete vision from within Father Mountain and he had been here only a bit over a century. Damon still required the use of the window to see outside, and would for hundreds of years to come.

Malic had been chosen for this mission because he was not yet a full Guardian, but a Guardian Aide. Most Guardian Aides, unlike Malic, were at one time Earth Kinder who had passed away and had gone to Heaven. It was considered a high honor to be selected by Otheon for the position of Guardian Aide, especially so for an Olinian. Otheon had been appointed by the Father, Himself, and had full reign over Ahveen, answering only to the Father.

Guardians are unknown to the Kinder by design. Unlike Guardian Angels, who work within a single time ring, Guardians have the ability to pass from one ring to any other to go to where they are needed. Guardians, unlike Guardian Angels, are active, physical participants in the lives of the Kinder they are assigned to.

Everyone has read about the family dog that dived into a freezing river to save its owner. *That* is what the Guardians do. They are transformers who can assume the identity of any living being, the family dog, a friend, whatever they find helpful at the time of crisis. Otheon monitors all times at all times and can dispatch a Guardian to where it is needed in time to save the worthy of the world. Being in complete control of time, Otheon can send a Guardian "after the fact" and yet, he always arrives just in time.

Guardian Angels, who the Kinder are aware of, are not physically active. The close call one has when a truck almost hits one's car is probably just a close call, rather than a tragic accident, because a Guardian Angel "whispered" in the ear of the truck driver, awakening him just in time. But, if one found oneself hanging from a cliff, ready to fall, and from nowhere a hand reached down, *that* was the hand of a Guardian.

The distinction is subtle, yet well defined. Guardian Angels reside in Heaven while Guardians reside in Ahveen. The efforts of Guardians have always been attributed to those of Guardian Angels, but that was all part of the design. Guardians have always been, and so remain, unknown to the Kinder. The one thing that a Guardian cannot do that a Guardian Angel can do, is intervene in a suicide. A Guardian Angel is free to try and dissuade a human from taking their life. A Guardian, being always physically active in their actions to save the Kinder, is not free to stop a suicide. The Father gave the Kinder free will and that gift is considered absolute. The gun cannot be grabbed away; the razor may not be removed from the wrist. Only persuasion is permitted, and that is the job of the Angels.

Damon reached the window and watched as Malic emerged from the portal and confronted the boys. Malic, being a mere Guardian Aide, could do what a Guardian was never permitted to do, openly reveal himself in a form other than that of a bobcat. Not all bobcats are Guardians, but all Guardians when outside Father Mountain, and not in transit to assignment, are bobcat in form. This rule also applied to Malic, but with the one exception that he was permitted to choose other forms when given the assignment of an aide, that of guarding and aiding the Guardians.

Malic, more so than other aides had developed the gift of choosing the one form that had always been effective to the task at hand. *That* is why Malic was sent to the boys. They posed a serious threat to the order of things and Malic was the Guardians' best hope of averting that threat.

Malic, unnoticed by the boys as they discussed their situation, approached silently, as only a bobcat could. It was Red who first noticed Malic about ten feet from him. Malic immediately stopped, sat down, and studied Red, going into his mind's memories.

"Jim...Look..." Red whispered.

Jim looked in the direction Red was pointing and saw Malic sitting, motionless before them.

"Where did he come from?" Jim asked.

"From the Lair, I think. He stopped there and sat down when I first looked over at him. He hasn't moved since," Red explained.

As the boys studied the bobcat, wondering what its next move might be, Malic began his transformation into his selected form.

"Damn, Jim! He's...he's...changing? What the hell is going on?"

"Jim just stared in disbelief. The bobcat was reshaping itself in a smooth, fluid manner, becoming less like a bobcat and more like a silvery ball. After about five seconds all that was left of the bobcat was a metallic looking ball, not solid in appearance, but like mercury, fluid and flowing within. Another five seconds produced another change, the silvery ball flowing into a rough human form and finally, within five more seconds a man appeared; a man Red recognized well.

"Gramps!" Red yelled. "Gramps, what are you doing here?—Jim, look, it's my grandpa!"

Malic smiled and extended his arms to Red.

"Hello, Red. Gad it's good to see you again. How have you been?" Malic said, imitating Red's Gramps perfectly.

"I've been fine, Gramps. How have you been?" Red asked, rushing to his embrace.

Malic hugged Red and patted him on the back, just as Red remembered his Gramps used to do.

"I've been good, Red. Gram said to give you a big hug when I saw you, so this is from her, too," Malic said, convincingly. "She's sorry she couldn't be here, but only one of us was permitted to come."

"Tell her I love her when you see her, Gramps. Don't forget. Come…come over here and sit down. Do you remember Jim?" Red asked.

"Sure. Hello Jim, how've you been, son?" Malic asked, smiling a warm smile.

"I've been fine, sir…you?"

"Just fine, although I do miss my loved ones here on Earth. But, Heaven is…well—Heaven is Heaven. It's just like I had hoped it would be. No more arthritis pain, I'm with Red's Grandma every day, and Red, her lumbago is all cleared up. It's grand!"

"That's great, Gramps. This is so great! God, it's good to see you again!"

"Well, Red. I'm here to help. I noticed you have a problem and I asked permission to come to your assistance. It seems you've gotten yourself into a bit of a bind," Malic said, resting his hand on Red's shoulder.

"I'll say, Gramps. We're stuck in the year 2087!"

"Now how did you manage that?" Malic asked.

"Jim found a map to this place called the Cats' Lair. It's some sort of door to the future, but apparently, *only* the future. We can't get back," Red explained. "Jim, show Gramps the map."

"No," Jim answered, flatly.

"Jim…What…?"

"Red, that's not your Gramps," Jim stated, bluntly.

"Sure it is, Jim, just look," Red answered, confused at Jim's behavior.

"Looking won't do any good, Red. I never met your grandfather—ever. He claimed to remember me and that's a lie. We *never* met. That's not your grandfather and he is not here to help," Jim cautioned.

"Sure he is, Jim," Red said, studying Malic closely. "It's Gramps."

"Then ask him what's on the back of your calf," Jim suggested. "If he's your Gramps he'll know…he'll remember."

Red thought about the birthmark on his calf while Malic read his thoughts of it.

"You mean the moon shaped birthmark, Jim?" Malic answered. "And—I do remember you. It is you that was too young to remember me, son. You were only about three years old, if I remember correctly."

"Clever. I don't know how you knew about the birthmark, but you had died before I ever met Red. What's your answer to that?" Jim demanded.

Malic hissed and then spoke harshly, "Leave this place and do not use the map again. Take it far away and dispose of it where it will never be found again. You do not know what you are dealing with and the damage you can do. GO! And do not return!"

More quickly than he had evolved into Red's grandfather, Malic transformed into his own form and stood before the boys.

"Gillespie!" Red exclaimed.

"My name is actually Malic, resident Aide of Father Mountain. I came to you at the diner to warn you away from here. Why did you not heed my warning? Did you think I was lying about the dangers? I was not. Now you are stuck here in a time totally unfamiliar to you. If you persist in experimenting with the portal, you will only bring more sorrow to yourselves. Leave this place and do not look back. Be content where you now find yourselves. It is your only option. There is no way back."

Malic turned abruptly and became the bobcat once again, leaping into the portal and vanishing.

"They've known we were coming since before we ever arrived in Clermont," Jim said, not quite understanding what it all meant.

"Damn, Jim. How did you know? I really thought that was Gramps. How did you know?" Red asked, as confused as he was disappointed.

"I didn't know for sure, but I knew you would be less able to tell than me, being emotional and all over his sudden appearance. So I tested him."

"But, he passed the test. He knew about the birthmark," Red said, still unsure of what he had missed that Jim had picked up on.

"Not that test. I did meet your grandfather—at your twelfth birthday party—remember. I *wasn't* too young to remember and he sure didn't die before I met you," Jim explained. If he had truly been your Gramps he would never have forgotten that day. I spilled grape juice all over his suit that afternoon, and he would know that I remembered it as well. I really wasn't sure, one way or the other, until he gave *himself* away," Jim explained.

*   *   *

Malic, disappointed in himself at not getting Red to volunteer the map, reported to Damon immediately upon his return.

"I'm sorry, Damon. I was tricked," Malic apologized. "I never got the chance to be offered the map and I didn't even have the opportunity to convince them, as the grandfather, to stay put in the time ring they are in. I had my whole strategy planned out, but that boy, Jim, tricked me."

"You were more than tricked, Malic; you were duped. Jim is clever, too clever. I fear he will eventually arrive at the solution to his return to 2002. Don't despair though, Malic. I think your plan would have worked well had Red been alone. We have never been confronted with two intruders arriving together. We will have to develop a better plan for such occasions in the future; if there is to be a future as we know it."

"Tell me, Damon, that I may understand. Why is their return to their own time such a bad thing? Your whole purpose as a Guardian is to help worthy Kinder in times of need. Are these boys not worthy?"

"Oh no, Malic. They are worthy of our compassion, and help, in any other circumstance. They are good boys who have done nothing wrong. It is what they may unwittingly do with their new knowledge that worries us. The knowledge is relatively harmless if they can go only forward, but to return home, to their ring of time, could be serious trouble for the world. You see, Malic, no one can predict the future and therefore no one can directly change it, not and be sure of the outcome. That's life as it is normally lived. Going forward in time is no different than lying down to sleep at night. When you awake in the morning you have awakened in the future. Take this as an example. A Kinder goes to bed at night, only to awaken to his house on fire and his children perished. Why did he not awaken in time? Because he had not put a new battery in his smoke alarm. If he could now return to the point in time when he went to bed, what would he do?"

"Put a new battery in the alarm," Malic stated.

"Excellent. So now the alarm goes off that night and he saves his children. But, he later discovers that his dog has perished in the blaze. What does he do now?" Damon asked.

"He goes back and lets the dog out for the night?" Malic guessed.

"Yes, he might do that in order to save the dog, or he might do what he should have done in the first place; turn off the space heater before retiring. You see, once Kinder can master time travel, there will never again be a permanent and unchangeable past."

"But, how does that pertain to the boys? If they get back home they will probably never enter the portal again."

"Probably not, but once they tell their tale, and bring people to see that they are not crazy by using the map to demonstrate the portal, the Kinder will not rest until they figure out how to duplicate it in every living room in the world. And fool yourself not, they will try and they are resourceful."

"Then why doesn't the Father simply stop them himself?" Malic asked.

"Because He gave them free will in the beginning and created no laws to govern the use of the portal. Therefore, in His eyes, they have done nothing wrong. The portal was never supposed to be discovered by the Kinder so there was no need of a law to prohibit its use by them. In fact, to have created a law such as that would have been counterproductive, drawing attention to it, just like the apple. Look what that cost them."

"I see. To tell them not to do something is to peak their curiosity and then, they are bound and determined to do it. Is that then—the true reason no law was written?"

"No, Malic. The reason was as I stated. It was not thought necessary. Many laws have been written that the Kinder, for the most part, obey faithfully. Then, there are others that disobey. That *is* free will."

"Then, Damon, what are we to do now?" Malic asked.

"We do nothing for now. We let them exercise their will and if they come to the solution, we will send you to reason with them and explain the great burden they will be carrying back to their time with them."

"I…Damon?"

"Yes, Malic…you. But, do not worry my friend. We will tell you what needs to be said if that time comes."

CHAPTER 11

The Solution?

*T*heir encounter with Malic had been interesting. The encounter had been very much more than just interesting though; it had been enlightening. Malic's intent, initially, had been to deceive the boys into being content with where they were in time. He had a carefully contrived story to use for this purpose, had he the time to convey it to them. He had not, and his temper had gotten the best of him, resulting in the use of a verbal warning, a threat with no substance.

What the boys took away from the encounter was a heightened curiosity about what, or who was behind the Lair and the appearance of Malic. Damon's sending Malic had had an opposite effect on the boys than intended. Now, they were determined to solve the riddle.

"Red, there is something strange about how these *beings* are handling us. They seem to have powers far beyond ours. They seem to have knowledge of things we have never even dreamed of. Yet, they make no attempt to simply stop us. They send bobcats with notes, they send someone impersonating your Gramps to deceive us, and they send Gillespie with his strange story of Carter Elliott. But, they do nothing to just physically stop us."

"It's almost as if they can't," Red commented. "Just like you thought before."

"Exactly," Jim confirmed. "I think they are powerless to interfere with us beyond trickery and lies. I think that this meeting confirms that theory."

"What if you're wrong, Jim?" Red asked, sheepishly.

"Then maybe we die. I don't know, but whatever they do can't be worse that staying here for the rest of our lives. We don't fit in here. I mean, it is cool, but it's not home. I'm willing to take my chances and try to get home—you?" Jim asked Red.

"I'm for it, too. I still want to fix things for Laura, and I can't do that here."

"You mean you want to *be* with Laura—and you're right—you can't do that here," Jim said, smiling and shoving Jim's shoulder. "So, let's get back to figuring this out. I don't buy for a minute that this is a one way street."

The boys sat on the ground facing one another; legs crossed in front of them and began discussing the possibilities. Red had pretty much figured out the timing involved and as complicated as it would be to figure out exactly how long to stay in the Lair to achieve a precise result, that of going to a specific hour or day in time, figuring out how to go to a particular year was feasible. The problem remained direction. The secret of how to go back in time was remaining just that, a secret, so far.

They discussed everything leading up to their first entry into the Lair. Then they discussed their first trip in and hit upon the words on the note; double reverse curvilineal. They now believed that *double* referred to the two time ratios involved and *curvilineal* meant that the tunnel is curved, not straight, as it appeared to be. *Reverse* must refer to the direction change. But how? In and of itself, the word did not explain how to reverse direction. It indicated only that reversing *may* be possible.

Jim was the first to come up with a theory.

"Red, maybe reverse doesn't refer to the direction traveled, but the way you enter the Lair. Maybe we should try backing in and backing out. You know, like in reverse, on a car. Back up the whole trip and maybe *we* back up in time."

"Hey! Maybe you're right! It's certainly worth a test. We need to go back the eight months we just moved forward, and then a little more to get to before we stripped the tree. We can back in for eighteen seconds and then backing out should then take eighteen minutes. If it works, we'll come out to find the bark on the tree back like it was before we stripped it."

"Or—we won't remember having stripped it. It just hit me, Red. What if by going back to before we stripped the bark, we are who we were then, armed only with the knowledge we had then. We won't have actually stripped the bark yet, so how would we remember ever doing it?"

"No, Jim. I don't buy that. That Malic guy, and whoever else is in that mountain, wouldn't be so damned worried about us figuring this out if we wouldn't remember ever being in the future in the first place. And, our getting back is what they are afraid of. I think that whatever we experience, *we* experience. If we go back to before we stripped the tree, we'll remember having done it. The fact that we don't need to do it again, and don't, is the point at which we first alter the future—*That* is what they are afraid of! It just hit me! They are afraid we will master this thing and learn to alter the future."

"How do you figure that?" Jim asked.

"Malic. Remember what he said? 'There is no way back'. They're afraid that if we get back we'll spill the beans about this place and someone will figure out how it all works."

"So, why don't they just stop us?"

"That, I don't know. That doesn't make sense to me either," Red agreed. "But, they have done nothing more than talk so far. Again, maybe that's all they can do."

"Well, let's give it another shot and hope you're right," Jim said.

They approached the Lair, turned and lowered themselves to their hands and knees. Red took the lead and began backing.

"Well, here goes. One Mississippi—Two Mississippi—Three Mississippi—Four   Mississippi—Five   Mississippi—Red   continued counting off the seconds…Seventeen Mississippi—Eighteen Mississippi—TURN!"

As they turned they found themselves instantly outside.

"What the hell? What happened to the eighteen minute crawl out of there?" Red asked, totally bewildered.

"Hell if I know," Jim replied.

❦   ❦   ❦

Damon laughed as he watched from the window.

"Ha! Malic, I am sure glad that we don't have to fool with those ratios," he confessed.

"As am I, Damon. We'd never get to where we needed to be if we did. This *is* funny, watching I mean."

"They are determined. I'll give them that."

"Why is it that we can go to whenever we want and they must—how did you put it—*fool* with those ratios?"

"When Caspeic created his map to overcome his problem of getting lost, we thought nothing of it as the map alone was worthless to the finder. It would lead only to a rock wall in a canyon. Without knowledge of the proper words to think, the portal would remain invisible to anyone who came there. Then one day, quite to our surprise, the Indian, Little Hawk, was discovered *in the portal*. It caught us by complete surprise. Of course, Caspeic was questioned because Little Hawk was in possession of the map. It was then that Caspeic informed us of having blessed the map with the power of passage. We went immediately to the Father and beseeched him to relocate the portal, but He said that the portal was where it was for a reason and it could not be moved. Instead, to make using the portal nearly impossible, he created the complex sets of time ratios involved for anyone from the outside coming in. He did this in an instant while Little Hawk was still in the portal. Without the *right* of passage, Little Hawk became instantly trapped in the complexities of the new time ratios."

"I see," Malic replied. "The interloper becomes so confused over the outcome of his venture that he eventually gives up trying to go back home."

"Exactly. But, of course, that creates a great deal of anxiety for the intruder and the Father saw that they lost all hope, all because of simple curiosity. So, he instructed us to always provide them with the clue we now give them. He knows that it is a risk, but each and every Kinder is important to Him and he felt that they must have hope, despite the risk."

Malic smiled as he began to understand and turned his attention, once again, to the boys' endeavors outside the portal.

❧   ❧   ❧

"So, if we lost the eighteen minutes coming out, where are we? I mean in what year are we?" Jim asked, making a good point.

"A little more than a day's difference from when we left, I guess. If we are still right about the timing." Red answered, rubbing his chin. "Is the scar still on the tree?"

"In one day's time it would be, in either direction we traveled. But—the tree's not there!" Jim cried, staring in disbelief.

"Oh shit!"

"Oh shit is right. Where did the frickin' tree go?"

"I guess it either died, fell and decayed, or it hasn't grown there yet," Red observed, speculating on their now very serious situation.

"Holy crap, Red! What the hell happened?"

"We went either very far back, or very far forward, somehow. That's all I can figure."

The boys slumped to the ground realizing that they had no idea where they were now. They sat silently for a moment, each trying to sort out what to do next.

Suddenly, Jim raised his head and sniffed the air, first in one direction and then another.

"Red, do you smell anything?" Jim asked. "Like someone grilling, maybe?"

Red sniffed the air.

"Yes, It does smell like someone's grilling. Where would that be coming from?"

"It's coming from the direction of the lake. Come on," Jim said.

Jim stood and walked toward the edge of the lake. As he broke free from the forest at the lake's shore he saw the source of the smell he and Red had noticed a moment ago. Red, who had followed Jim to the shore stood beside him.

"Damned if we didn't do it. We went *back*. By God, we went back!" Red exclaimed.

"Yeah—we went back all right. Too far back!"

Jim and Red were staring at a sight that no living man from their original time had ever seen. There before them, just across the lake, was a real Indian village. There were children running about, playing, and women washing clothes at the lake's edge. Further out in the lake there was one person who appeared to be bathing. They saw several cook fires blazing with what appeared to be deer carcasses suspended above them. There were about twenty dwellings in all constructed of pine boughs and poles. Smoke hung in the still air just above the village like a white blanket covering all and creating a surreal appearance to the scene they were witnessing.

"Damn, Red. We went back all right. Look at that! Did you ever in your life think you'd see something like this?" Jim marveled.

"No, and I'm not too happy to be seeing it now. We better get the hell out of sight though, before they see us. They may be hostile."

"I don't think so, Red. I think we are back to before any white men ever came to these parts. Look. None of them are wearing any kind of cloth. It's all buckskins and such. And—look at the men. None of them are carrying rifles. The ones that are armed at all have bows slung across their shoulders. There are no cook pots on the fires either. There doesn't appear to be anything over there that would have come from trading with white men. I think we are here before that time," Jim explained.

"Well then—I don't want to be the first white man they meet. There's no telling how that might turn out. Let's get back into the trees, now, and figure out the timing to go forward again."

As they crept back into the trees, Jim asked, "How far? We've lost our reference point now. It could be 1500 or 1600 or 1700 for all we know. Maybe even before that! How far forward do we go?"

Red explained his new plan as they walked back toward the Lair.

"We'll time it for one hundred years the first trip. We know how to do that, at least. We'll check for our tree when we come out," Red explained.

Neither of the boys relished the idea of what they were up against. Their first trip forward of eighty-four years had required over thirty-six hours in the Lair. This trip would last nearly two days and the thought of the pain and discomfort involved was almost enough to discourage them from trying. But, what else were they to do? They would surely not survive long in this time period. For all they knew, they were the only two white men on the entire continent right now. It was a terribly frightening thought, which completely overshadowed their distaste for spending two days in the Lair.

Red worked out the timing involved and the boys crawled into the Lair. They emerged into the forest roughly forty-three hours later, and they hoped, one hundred years closer to home. They were thirsty and tired and bruised terribly about their hands and knees, but at least they had made it back out. Luckily, once again, they exited the Lair into warm weather. It was apparently summer in whatever year they were in.

Much to their dismay, their tree was still missing from the forest. They proceeded to the lake's edge to check out the village and found it deserted and in a serious state of disrepair, the dwellings having mostly fallen down into piles of decaying pine matter. The Indians had been long gone from this place, but the fact that the remnants of their existence were still present told the boys they had further to go. They drank profusely from the lake and wished that they had some food to eat. Having drank all that they could hold, they returned to the Lair.

"Let's get some sleep, Red. We'll just have to try again after we rest up a bit. Unfortunately, we don't have the luxury of resting for too long if we are going to get back before we starve to death."

"Back to when?" Red asked, having become quite discouraged. "Maybe we should walk back down to Clermont and see if it is there yet. We could get food there and rest our hands and knees before coming back and trying again," he suggested.

"And what if Clermont isn't there? What if the access road and highway are not there yet? We'll get hopelessly lost in the forest. I don't think we can take that chance," Jim advised.

"I guess you're right. So what then? Another hundred years?" Red asked Jim.

"I'd say at least that. When we first came up here in 2002 there was absolutely no sign of that village. Nothing. It would have taken a very long time to have completely weathered away to nothing, not a trace. I'd say at least one hundred more years, maybe two."

"But two hundred years would mean nearly four days in the Lair. Four days without water and we're dead, or nearly so. I think we'll have to settle for one hundred years at a time, max. You agree?" Red asked.

"Yeah—I do. You're right. Let's get some sleep and we'll do it again in a few hours."

❦   ❦   ❦

Damon watched with great interest. The persistence of the boys was both troubling and rewarding for Damon. The spirit of the Kinder was not easily broken and this pleased him. But, what would their spirit and persistence mean to the future of their race? This was the troubling aspect of the drive the boys displayed. Damon found himself rooting the boys on and at the same time wishing they would simply declare that they had had enough and give in. They had inadvertently shot themselves back into the early 1700's and had now come back to 1830. One more one hundred year leap and they would run the distinct possibility of—*Well, I'd rather not think about that,* Damon thought. *That would definitely be interesting, to say the least.* He watched as the boys bedded down on the forest floor, and smiled. *Interesting, indeed.*

❦   ❦   ❦

Red awoke six hours later, momentarily forgetting when, or where he was. As he shook the sleep from his head his predicament came back to him instantly. He rolled over and shook Jim into consciousness.

"Jimbo. Wake up. It's time to try again."

Jim rubbed his eyes and yawned, and trying to come back from dreams of better times, answered, "Damn, Red. I was back home at the foundry. I was never so glad to be at work in my life!"

"Well, if we get through another two days in the Lair, maybe we will be back home enjoying a lot more than the foundry. I'm thinking *steak*! T-bone steak!"

Standing and dusting himself off, Jim replied, "Then let's do it. 2002, here we come—I hope."

As much as they hated to have to do it, the boys once again crawled into the Cats' Lair, this time with even higher hopes of coming out in the year 2002, or at least close enough to it to consider it home again. Like the previous voyage into the Lair, they were not met by any messengers bearing notes or other warnings. It seemed as though they were being left to their own devices, free to venture from one time to another. Jim's theory that the powers within the mountain were not at liberty to, or unable to physically stop them, seemed to be ringing true as they had not been stopped or interfered with on either trip. They hoped it would remain that way until they jumped this next one hundred years ahead.

As they crawled from the Lair this time, they were glad to see that their luck was holding out as to the season that greeted them. Once again the air was warm and dry. They quickly scrambled to their feet and went to check on their tree.

They stood at the spot where the tree they had marked should have been, but again it was not there.

"We're too early, again. But how early?" Red asked.

"No. Wait, Red. If the tree was here we would have overshot our mark. That tree was no more than fifty years old, or about that. We stripped the bark in 2086. Take away fifty years and we are back in our future again, 2036, approximately."

"Right! We don't want to find the tree now, do we? We want to be back to before the tree grew here. Still, how much before it grew here are we?—I'm going to get a drink."

Jim followed and when they reached the shore they looked out across the water to the area where the village had been. It was as it had been when they had first arrived. All traces of the village were gone. Time had taken it away just as surely as it had taken away their lives. Jim thought about that and a tear ran down his cheek.

Damon watched and felt badly for them. If only they had not let their curiosity get the better of them. But, how were they to know where it would lead them? It was about time to send Malic to them again. They were getting close now and if they guessed right and made a forty-year jump out of fear of overshooting their mark, their next trip would bring them very close to where they wanted to be. If they jumped much more than that, or made a second jump, Damon feared the worse for the boys, and that, he really didn't want to see. But, it would solve the whole problem for the Guardians. If they did make just one shorter jump, Malic would have to go to them and explain the ramifications of their actions beyond that point in time. They would have to be informed of the need for total secrecy about the portal. Once they knew the full potential of their actions, perhaps they would voluntarily relinquish the map to Malic. That, at least was his hope.

Damon was just about to turn from the window to go to Malic when he noticed movement in the forest behind the boys. He turned his attention back to the window.

"Oh no," he muttered under his breath. "It can't be. What are the chances of this?" he asked himself, not expecting an answer. His previous fears had come to pass, and now, even he wasn't sure what to expect.

Wiping the tear from where it hung from his chin, Jim leaned forward and drank his fill of the cool lake water. Red was already indulging himself, gulping down mouthfuls as fast as he could swallow them. Never had water tasted so good, or refreshing. If there were nothing else to be thankful for, the fact that the Lair was located at this lake was at least one thing to be grateful for.

Having drank their fill, once again the boys stood and headed back for the Lair, fulfilled, yet not. Suddenly, Jim stooped behind a large stump, motioning for Red to do likewise. Something had moved in the forest to their right. Jim had barely noticed it in his peripheral vision, but something had been there, he was sure.

"Red, someone's over there," he said, pointing in the general direction of the movement. "I saw something move over there. Not sure what or who, but something's there."

Red squinted and stared into the area Jim had indicated. Then, he saw movement, too. Through the trees about fifty yards away, something glided between the trees. All he could make out was a flash of color; red above blue, then it was gone. They began creeping ahead on their bellies, stalking the intruder in *their* valley. They could now see that whoever, or whatever it was, had stopped. They crawled closer and the form of a man wearing blue overalls and a red plaid shirt came into view. He was also wearing a hat and backpack and was stooped over something on the ground.

"Do you see him," Red asked.

"Yeah, I see him. What's he looking at?" Jim asked, trying to make it out for himself.

Just then, the man reached down and picked something up from the ground.

"It looks like a piece of paper," Red commented.

Suddenly, the conversation at the diner with Gillespie shot through Jim's head.

Red plaid shirt and overalls, raced through Jim's mind. *Carter Elliott!* He grabbed for his shirt pocket. It was still buttoned, but the map was gone!

"Red," Jim whispered in a panic. "That's Elliott! He's found the map. The Indian did drop it here after all!"

"You've got the map. How can that be?" Red asked, looking over at Jim in confusion.

"No—I don't have it any more," he whispered. "Think about it. He hasn't buried it at the farm yet. He hasn't even been into the Lair yet. Shit Red, it's 1930 and he's just now finding that map!"

"Then he has no idea what it is. Come on; let's see if we can get it from him. We'll tell him we dropped it there and thank him for finding it for us," Red blurted out, scrambling for an idea. He knew far to well that without the map he and Jim were stuck in 1930 and would be very old men by the time 2002 came around again, *if* they lived that long.

"Hold on, Red. Let's think about this for a minute. He won't be going anywhere for a while. He still has to go back to the Clermont Café and ask around about the Cats' Lair before coming back up here to look. Remember what Gillespie told us?"

"Yes, I remember and I also remember that he told us that it was 1990 before he returned to the café. If he gets into the Lair with that map, we'll have to wait sixty years before we'll have a chance to get it back. We'll be eighty years old by then!" Red exclaimed. "That *won't* do, Jim. We've got to get it now!"

❦   ❦   ❦

Damon grimaced at what he was witnessing. This was the boys' first opportunity to rewrite history and they were seriously considering it. In fact, it appeared that they were determined to do so, come hell or high water. This was what Damon had feared from the very first day he had set eyes on these two. Their persistence and stubbornness, which he had recognized immediately, was about to lead to the first altering of what history had cast. This was the unknown, even to the Guardians. He shuddered and turned, screaming as he did, "Malic! Malic! Come here Malic, NOW!"

Moments later, Malic entered the windowed chamber on the run.

"What is it, Damon? What is wrong?"

"The boys are about to alter the path of history. They have unwittingly arrived back in the forest in 1930 at the precise time that Carter Elliott has just found the map. I know, what are the odds of that happening? But it has! They have discovered that they no longer possess the map and are determined to get it back. We need to intervene now. There is not a moment to spare."

"But, Damon, what can I do?" Malic asked, completely at a loss for a solution.

"Look," Damon said, directing Malic's attention to the window. "As the boys are discussing what to do next, Carter Elliott is moving away into the forest. Go immediately there and assume the farmer's form. Get between him and the boys. *Be* Carter Elliott when they come to you, thus delaying them while the real Carter Elliott makes his way back to Clermont. Use your imagination and delay them from their chosen course. Go, now! Waste not another minute!"

Malic *melted* into the form of the bobcat and ran from the room. Moments later, Damon saw him emerge from the portal and reform as Carter Elliott, disappearing into the forest. Damon refocused his line of sight to the boys, who were still discussing what they would do next. Carter Elliott was now over the ridge and heading for Clermont. He relaxed and smiled a small smile. It now appeared that Malic would have time to intervene.

Damon started to enter the falls, then stopped. Suddenly something occurred to him that totally perplexed him. *How, if the boys had lost possession of the map by traveling back prior to Carter Elliott's having buried it, did they enter the portal back in the 1700's and 1800's? Is it possible that passing their original birth dates by traveling back to before they were actually born made need of the map unnecessary? After all, no Kinder has ever done that before. Perhaps, just perhaps, they have become nonbeings, not in true existence yet and therefore free to enter at will.* Damon found these thoughts to be very interesting, yet quite disturbing. He would have to see if Otheon knew the answers to these questions. One thing was apparently certain. The boys no longer needed the map. He hoped they would not also figure that out.

❦   ❦   ❦

Malic sat down on a log and waited for the boys to arrive. He began thinking about how he would handle this new situation. There had not been time for Damon to brief him with ideas that might be helpful. He was on his own and the course of history remaining undisturbed was resting in his hands. As he sat there thinking, an idea began to form. Malic smiled and went to work on his idea. It was a simple thing for him to do. He was a transformer and that power extended to inanimate objects if he so desired. He looked around and picked up a pinecone. Holding it firmly grasped in his closed hand he closed his eyes and concentrated. When he opened his hand he smiled. *Not bad,* he thought. *Pretty good replica of Caspeic's map.* He laughed softly and waited.

"Come on, Jim," Red coaxed. "He's gone toward the access road, but we can still catch up to him before he gets back to his car."

Red took off at a trot toward the road with Jim following reluctantly. Jim had wanted to think it through before acting, but Red was not going to be stopped. For some reason, Jim realized that taking the map from Carter Elliott might create changes in the future that would adversely effect them, somehow. He didn't know how, but that is why he wanted time to think about it. Red, on the other hand, didn't see beyond the fact that without the map there was no way back to 2002, other than growing old waiting for it to arrive.

"Red, wait," Jim said, calling ahead to Red. "Let's just think about this a minute."

"Think about what, Jim? There is nothing to think about. We *need* that map, period," Red yelled back to him without slowing down a step.

"I don't know what there is to think about, but there may be something we are overlooking."

Jim stopped. Red looked back at him and pulled up also, turning and walking back to him.

"Like what, then?" Red asked.

"Well—For one, he doesn't buy this mountain because it isn't special to him without knowing that the Lair is here. Maybe his not buying it allows development of the mountain into a ski resort or something. Maybe a building gets built over the portal. I don't know, but I do know that whatever we do we better think it through. There may be a lot we can do wrong to screw ourselves up if we're not careful."

"I don't think so. One more short trip into the Lair and we're back home where we want to be, that's all there is to it. But, we need the map to do that. So quit stalling and let's get moving."

Red turned and started a slow run along the route Carter Elliott had taken. Jim shook his head and followed, despite his misgivings he realized that they had to stick together. After all, about all they had in this world was each other. A hundred yards later, Red stopped abruptly. There, sitting on a log, was Carter Elliott.

Red was the first to approach, cautiously at first, and then with more confidence as he settled on what he would say to Mr. Elliott. Jim followed close behind Red, ready to back up whatever story he was about to contrive.

"Hi there!" Red hailed.

Malic looked up and smiled.

"Hello. Where'd you boys come from?" he asked.

"We're camped over by the lake, you?" Red asked.

"Oh. I'm out here from Illinois looking to buy some ranch land. Today though, I'm just exploring the area, sort of relaxing and enjoying the scenery," Malic lied.

"Really! We're from Illinois also. We came out here because of a map we found showing this mountain and a place called the Cats' Lair," Red said, truthfully.

"Is that so. Would this be the map?" he asked, showing Red the map he had just created.

Red looked at the map feigning surprise as he reached into his shirt pocket and made an obvious attempt to locate his map.

"Yes, that's it. Where'd you get that? I must have dropped it without realizing it," Red explained, twisting the truth.

"I found it on the ground back there aways. So these words on here mean the Cats' Lair, huh?" Malic asked Red.

"Yes, and Father Mountain. They're French. We looked them up at the library back home and then got curious about this place, so we came out to explore the mountain and look for the Cats' Lair," Red explained.

"Have you found this Cats' Lair yet?" Malic asked.

"Yeah, it's just an old cave. There are a lot of bobcats in the area where it's located. I guess that's where the name comes from," Red explained, totally fabricating an answer that he hoped would leave Mr. Elliott satisfied that there was nothing much to the map of interest.

Malic smiled and handed the map to Red.

"Well, here's your map back. That sounds like an interesting place, but I don't have the time today to see it. I've got to get back to town and close on the property I'm buying," Malic said, standing and brushing off the seat of his overalls. "Nice meeting you."

"Yeah, you to, sir," Red answered.

Jim who had been watching and listening silently, nodded and smiled at Malic, raising his open hand in a waving gesture. "See ya," he muttered.

"Say, before you go," Red said, stopping Malic's departure. "You wouldn't have any grub in your pack that you could spare us, would you? We've been up here so long that we ran out of supplies. We're getting rather hungry."

Malic smiled and removed his pack.

"Sure," he answered, and reaching into the pack produced a couple of apples and bananas. "I hope this will do," he said. "I eat mainly fruits and vegetables."

"That'll do just fine!" Red stated, smiling broadly. "Thanks!"

Malic handed the fruits to Red and walked off into the forest. Red and Jim turned and started back to the Lair. As they walked they discussed their encounter with Carter Elliott between bites of the much welcomed and needed food.

"That went rather well," Red said, in a relaxed tone.

"Yes, for now," Jim replied.

"What's that supposed to mean?"

"It means that you just altered history. Now Mr. Elliott will never find the Lair and he will never buy this mountain. Don't be surprised if the next time we come out of the Lair there are bulldozers and backhoes up here tearing the place apart, that's all," Jim warned.

"You don't know that."

"No, but I'll tell you what I do know. Carter Elliott will not live until 2050 like he did the first time around. Odds are he'll die around 1990 having lost his sixty years in the Lair. What affect will that have upon the world? And, he was originally missing from the world from 1930 until 1990. Now, he'll be here. How will *that* affect the world?"

"I don't know, Jim, and I don't really care right now. What I do know is that I am not prepared to stay here and grow old before I was ever born. That's what I do know!" Red admonished.

They walked on in silence until reaching the Lair. Red sat down and stretched out on the pine needles.

"Look, Jim. We're both tired and I, for one, am not ready for another day and a half of crawling through that tunnel. We've got the map back, so let's just rest a while, get some much needed sleep and start fresh into the Lair tomorrow. How does that sound to you?"

"It sounds like you are finally coming to your senses," Jim kidded. "I'm all for letting my knees rest before starting again."

"Good. Then it's settled. We'll start tomorrow morning and by tomorrow evening we'll be back in our own world and we'll celebrate by ordering two giant T-bones at the Hummingbird Café. How's that sound to you?" Red asked, smiling at the thought of real food.

"*That*—sounds like a plan!" Jim returned, also relishing the though of a juicy steak.

Jim stretched out beside a little sapling pine a few feet from Red, and soon, both boys were sound asleep.

❦   ❦   ❦

"Very nicely done, Malic," Damon said, praising Malic's ingenuity. "Now Carter Elliott is still on his true course. Intervention is indeed your middle name. And I loved how you produced fruit from thin air! I didn't know you were *that* good at transforming."

"Nor did I, Damon. When I reached into that pack I wasn't sure what I would pull out, if anything. I've never tried transforming air into anything before. No one was more surprised than I when I found the fruit in there!"

"Now you've given Carter Elliott time to follow through on what he originally did with the map's discovery. We'll have to watch closely that the boys don't interfere with him when he returns. That will be my responsibility, however, to keep a close watch on things. The boys are sleeping now and Carter is well on his way back to Clermont. Go ahead and get some rest, Malic. I'll call you if and when I need you."

"Yes, Damon. I'll be ready," Malic replied, and left the windowed chamber for his own quarters.

Damon turned back to the window and watched as the boys slept peacefully. He smiled at the thought of their persistence and determination. He smiled more broadly at the thought of their ingenuity and cleverness.

"I am sorry boys, that things must be the way they are, but there is the future to protect," he whispered to them. A tear formed at the corner of his eye and removing it to the tip of his finger, Damon stared at it in disbelief. *I...*Damon did not finish the thought, but turned his attention instead, to what lay ahead. Malic would still have one last job to do. Malic would have to go to them one last time before they returned to civilization. He would have to forewarn them of the dangers of tampering with the future and disclosing the secret of the portal.

As he watched the boys sleep, the troublesome thought of the boys' free entry into the portal occurred to him again. Somehow they had been able to enter the portal in the distant past, without possession of the map. *How could that be?* he wondered again. *Had they somehow circumvented the protections in place by traveling back to before the map's creation?* Damon was confused for the first time in his afterlife. *Now,* he thought. *They believe they have the map once again, and in their minds, the boys now have no reason to believe they cannot enter.*

Malic's clever plan to divert the boys from retrieving the actual map had produced for them a placebo; a reason to believe they could once again enter the portal. That in mind they might try again, and perhaps, gain access despite the map's lack of true power. Would they be successful? Damon had no idea at this point. Everything now occurring was new territory, yet unexplored. Even though it was 1930 for them outside, if Carter Elliott enters the portal ahead of them then his eventual burying of the map is set in motion, but the map would be in transit for sixty years. Would this somehow prevent the boys from entering? When they had entered the portal in the 1700's and 1800's the map did not even exist, as Caspeic had drawn the map in late 1850. Perhaps the existence of the map, or its presence in the portal, would prohibit the boys' entry. Only *time* would tell.

Damon turned from the window and then glanced back at Jim sleeping peacefully in the forest. It had just occurred to him that Jim seemed to be at the beginning of understanding already. *That's good,* he thought, and turned away again crossing the chamber to his writing desk. He began recording the day's events in his journal:

> *There is much I do not understand about the back traveling these boys have now embarked on. What I do understand is that co-existence has no existence. The boys cannot be permitted to reenter their own time at any point other than a point in time after which they originally departed. Malic has unwittingly made his request for*

their salvation out of admiration for them, but in my opinion, if approved, fulfillment of his request will prove to be our solution and salvation. Now that they have preceded themselves in the world they must remain there. For them to proceed into their time before Otheon decides in favor of Malic's request would be to lose them forever.—My thoughts are troubled over these troubled times...

Damon returned to the window to await Carter Elliott's return to the portal.

❦   ❦   ❦

Much to Jim's approval, the weather had remained clear and warm throughout the night. He awoke to a beautiful summer morning beneath a clear blue sky. He rolled over to face Red and discovered that Red had left his pallet of pine needles and was nowhere to be seen.

Damn! Where did he go? Jim wondered. *Surely not into the Lair—alone?*

Just then, Red walked out from the surrounding forest.

"Morning, Jimbo. Went for a drink," Red stated, sitting down beside Jim.

"Good morning—You had me worried for a minute. I thought for a minute there you might have left without me—to the future, or the present, or whatever."

"Naw, I wouldn't do that. What would I do in there without you?" Red asked, chuckling and grinning, apparently in a pretty good mood. "That wouldn't be any fun. I'd miss you and your crazy ideas, like this one—that landed us here."

"Yeah, right," Jim countered. "I'll bet you would."

"Why don't you go over to the lake and get a big drink and then we'll get started when you get back," Red suggested.

"Okay, sounds good to me. That apple and banana didn't go too far. I'm starving and the thought of those T-bones waiting for us sounds really good right about now!"

Jim rose and started in the direction of the lake.

"Hey, Jim. Wait up. I think I'll go with you. I want to walk around the other side of the lake where the village used to be. Scratch around in the dirt over there and maybe we'll find some arrowheads or something. That would be cool to bring back some stuff that came from a real Indian village that we actually saw. Don't you think that'd be cool?" Red asked.

"Yeah, that would be cool. Let's try it."

Jim filled his belly with cool lake water and then they hiked around to the far shore where at one time, they knew the village had existed. They scuffed the soil searching for any artifacts that may have been left behind by the villagers who had once lived, played and worked on this very spot. Their efforts uncovered several obsidian arrow points and what Jim thought to be a bannerstone, which some archeologists believe to have been status symbols among the ancients.

All in all, the boys were quite delighted with their finds. There was simply something special about these artifacts because they had actually *seen* the people who had created them, first hand. Their uneasiness with being in a time that wasn't their own was temporarily put aside by the excitement of their discoveries in the soil of the long ago decayed and vanished village.

"This is so cool, Jimbo, but I think maybe we better get back to the Lair and try to get home," Red suggested.

Jim agreed wholeheartedly and they departed the old village site and began the hike around the lake to the Lair. They had slept rather late and had spent several hours on the opposite shore. It was now early afternoon as the Lair's location came into view. The boys suddenly stopped side-by-side and stared in disbelief.

"What's he doing back up here?" Red asked.

"Hell if I know, but he's looking awfully close at the Lair. You don't suppose he followed a bobcat and saw it go in there, do you?" Jim asked Red, speculating on what Carter was staring at so intently.

"Hell, how could he? You have the map and if we're right about it he couldn't possibly have seen that happen. You need the map—I think."

"Maybe without the map you can see something like that happen, but you can't follow. Maybe if you just happen to be watching, you'll see them enter, but that's it. Then you're left with the impossible tale to tell, which no one will believe. Maybe that's how it works," Jim offered in explanation.

They watched as Carter Elliott got down on his hands and knees and slowly crawled into the Lair, vanishing before their eyes. They stood, dumbfounded and staring at each other.

"How…? How did he do that? We've got his map—don't we?" Jim asked.

Red checked his shirt pocket.

"Yeah, it's right here," he said, patting his pocket.

"Then how did he go in?"

The boys rushed to the Lair and tried to follow Carter Elliott in. They crawled straight into the rock face of the cliff behind.

"Where is the frickin' tunnel?" Red screamed.

"I don't know!" Jim screamed back at him.

They stood up in what should have been the tunnel of the Lair and spun in circles looking for an explanation to their failure to enter. Red unbuttoned his shirt pocket and pulled out the map, unfolding it as quickly as his fingers would respond to his request. He gawked at it in total dread and despair.

"It's blank! It's frickin' blank!" he yelled. Red paused for a long moment; thinking while Jim examined the blank piece of old yellowed paper. "Malic!" Red yelled. "Malic, you son of a bitch!"

Jim now got the drift of what Red had just realized. Malic had come to them, this last time, as Carter Elliott. He had succeeded in tricking them this time and had trapped them in 1930.

"Shit!" Jim screamed. "Why? Why did you do this to us, Malic?"

"Because, you had to be stopped from tampering with what has already been cast as the future," Malic answered from a few feet away.

He had materialized without the boys having noticed and was seated, cross-legged, at the edge of the forest.

"Come and sit," he instructed. "There is much I have to tell you."

"Tell us? Tell us what? That you've trapped us here in a time before we were ever born! Carter Elliott has gone in with our map! Without it we are permanently stuck here! Shit, Malic, what have you got to tell us that we don't already know?" Red asked, exploding on Malic.

Malic smiled at Red. He understood the anguish he and Jim must be going through and he let Red's outburst roll off his back.

"Please, Red—Jim, come sit with me. There is much I have to explain."

Although reluctantly, the boys joined Malic on the ground, each sitting cross-legged facing each other, each a corner of the triangle they formed on the forest floor. Malic explained to them that nothing about their situation was permanent. He explained that they were close enough to their own time to age into it.

"Yes, but I'll be fifty years old by the time my life in that time begins! How is that supposed to make me feel?" Red questioned, still quite disturbed with Malic and his treachery.

"Me, too," Jim affirmed.

"Jim. You seem to understand a little about the sanctity of the future that has been cast by the past. You seem to have a beginning understanding that it should not be disturbed. I know you realize that you came to this spot of your own free will, that you entered the portal of your own free will. Now, your free will has cast you in a role that is distasteful to you, but who is truly responsible for that?" Malic asked.

"I guess we are," answered Jim.

"Yes, you are. The Father let you keep the gift of your free will throughout this whole adventure of yours. Damon and myself were at liberty only to misdirect and trick you along the way to prevent your learning how to travel back. We failed in our endeavors. Now, we are forced to reveal ourselves that you will understand the nature of what you jeopardize by returning to a time prior to where you have been on this journey."

"The Father? Damon?" Jim asked, puzzled.

"Let me explain it to you this way, Jim. When you were five years old you noticed that your mother had not latched the door to your basement. You went to the door and opening it, stood at the top of the stairs. You leaned forward to better see down into the basement you had never visited before and lost your balance. Do you remember this?" Malic asked.

"Yes—Yes, I do, now that you mention it," Jim responded, intrigued with the story he had lived as a child.

"You began to fall headlong down the stairs, but before you struck them for the first time you were pulled back to the top and out of the doorway. The door slammed shut and the latch fell into place. Do you remember *that*?"

"Yes. It scared me. I remember that well!" Jim exclaimed.

"Who do you suppose pulled you back from serious injury or possible death that day?" Malic asked sternly.

"Was it you?" Jim asked.

"No. I am only an aide. It was Damon, now second in charge of the Guardians."

"Guardians? You mean like Guardian Angels?" Red asked, getting into the conversation.

"No, they are different. The Guardians are like the fail-safe beings to the Guardian Angels. Had your Guardian Angel been present, Jim, you would have been warned to stay away from the door in the first place and you would have heeded the advice. In the absence of your

Guardian Angel you ventured to the brink of death and it was up to a Guardian, at that point, to save you. Damon did just that."

The boys were silent. Malic continued.

"Father Mountain is home to the Guardians and aides like myself. We live within the mountain in a place called Ahveen. The portal is our avenue into all times at any precise moment of our choosing. We are a closely guarded secret and the deeds we perform are generally attributed to Guardian Angels, whose presence is known to many of you here on Earth. When the Father sent his Son to Earth he was instructed to make no mention of the Guardians in His teachings. We were to remain a secret for all time. Up until now, our presence has gone undetected, but you two are the first of the few who have ventured into the portal to have the stamina and determination to learn how to travel back. This would have posed a problem had you been able to remain and demonstrate the use of the map to others."

"Well, why didn't you just take the map? Surely you could have," Jim asked.

"Because of your free will, which we can not violate. We had to relieve you of it of your own free will. Fortunately, you deprived yourselves of it by traveling back prior to its creation. I only intervened to prevent you from tricking it away from Carter Elliott when you returned to 1930. That brings me to my point. Damon knows how clever you are and he knows that you know where to find the map again after Carter Elliott buries it in 1992. Damon's two requests are that you leave the map buried there and that you simply keep our secret. You will not be able to prove it until the map is free to be found again, but still, Damon would like your word that you will keep Ahveen a secret."

"Why? I mean I'll agree to that, but why does it concern you if we can't prove the story?" Jim asked, curious about why such individuals would be worried over such a tale as they might tell.

"Because many religious people would choose to believe you out of faith alone. They would flock to this spot and be witness to our coming and going. As you have discovered, the portal can be seen to work, even when one cannot use it oneself. After enough people witness the comings and goings of the bobcats, the scientists would eventually show up. One day your technology will advance to the point where your scientists will figure out the complexities of the portal and try to duplicate it. If they are successful then time will have no meaning any longer. Whoever has control of the technology will have the power to play with the future at will. You can see what that might mean for the well being of mankind, can't you? In the wrong hands it could be disastrous. That is why your secrecy is so very critical to your race. Do you understand?" Malic asked in finishing.

Red shook his head in understanding. Jim did likewise, but asked, "Why bobcats?"

"Ha!" Malic laughed. "Because they are indigenous and generally move about undetected. That is why we use their form to come and go, that, and the fact that they can travel through the portal swiftly. It is only one rod long you know, so a bobcat can be down it in no time."

"What? That's impossible," Jim stated. "It took us days to crawl through it! A rod is only—ah…"

"About sixteen feet," Malic informed him. "Perceptions, Jim. The portal is curvilineal only to those who do not possess the right of passage. Caspeic, the Guardian who drew the map, bestowed it with the power of passage, but the right of passage remained within him as a Guardian. You see, a Guardian can merely think of the spot he wishes to be and the time he wishes to be there. He transforms into the form of the bobcat traveling swiftly down the portal into the world. Once into the forest he assumes his own form and travels at the speed of light to the location he has chosen. He always arrives in time because he controls time to within a few minutes of an event."

"So," Jim interrupted. "When Damon saw me start to fall down the stairs…"

"He focused on a point in time before you became aware of the unlatched door, raced through the portal bounding into the forest, reassumed his form and at the speed of light rushed to your side. He was actually there as you first noticed the door was unlatched, but not being a Guardian Angel he was forced to wait until there was immanent danger before acting," Malic explained. "That is the role of a Guardian."

The three sat for several more hours, discussing and learning, the boys about Ahveen, and Malic, about the Kinder. It was as interesting to Malic as it was to the boys. He had not had the chance to talk one on one with humans before, other than in the course of his duties. Those times had been rare, and he had always been cast in the role of the deceiver. This was different and enlightening.

"Malic, where do the Guardians come from? I mean, who are they, exactly?" Red asked.

"Most of them are deceased Kinder who went to Heaven and were then selected by Otheon for this duty. Some, like myself, are from other worlds, but the circumstances leading to becoming a Guardian or a Guardian Aide are the same."

"Other worlds?" Jim asked.

"Certainly. The Father has many worlds He created and watches over. Earth is but one of these worlds."

"And—Where are you from, Malic?" Jim asked, very interested in this enlightenment.

"Olin, a planet not unlike Earth in many respects. It is a lovely place," Malic answered. "It is at the far end of the Milky Way."

Red thought for a moment, and then asked, "Why did you get sent to Earth?"

"Olinians develop different skills as Guardians than do Earth Kinder. It is done to achieve a variety of talents among Guardians in each world," Malic explained.

"Do you do this forever, then?" Jim asked.

"No. We are eventually retired back to Heaven and replaced by new Guardians."

They finished up their conversation with both Red and Jim agreeing to keep the secret of the Guardians. Red did make one last plea to return to their appropriate time, now that they understood and agreed to remain silent about what they had learned. Malic replied with a riddle:

> *"Time will repair all injustices.*
> *Let time take care of your desires, and given time, all will be as it was.*
> *Co-existence has no existence."*

With those words spoken, Malic became the bobcat and trotted off into the portal.

The boys looked at each other, smiled, and headed for the access road. Just over the ridge was the beginning of their new lives. What they had just learned filled them with a new peace, and they were content with their new lives before their time.

Along the way back to Clermont they decided to remain in Colorado. They would begin new lives here, find jobs and start over. Eventually, fifty years from now, Laura would be born and they would visit her and her aunt. Of course, they would be unknown to both Laura and Aunt Laura, but as citizens of Clermont they would get the opportunity to see people they knew from their old existence. They would get to watch her grow up into the beautiful lady she would become. To Red, this was some small consolation for the life he might have had with her. But as she would turn twenty, he would be turning ninety, just a friendly old man who had been around town all her life.

The access road came into view and the boys picked up their pace into their new futures.

The Interim

*T*he decision to remain in Clermont had turned out to be a good one for Red and Jim. They *drifted* into town in August of 1930 on the pretense that they had hitchhiked west from Illinois to look for gold. They took jobs where they could find them, working for local ranchers and shopkeepers during the more inclement weather and as house painters during the summer season.

They purchased gold pans, picks and shovels and camping gear for their sojourns into the mountains. Their explanation for having come to town actually led to the reality of them becoming prospectors. They would work the odd jobs for the locals to finance their mining trips and then, when they had enough to make their stake, they would disappear into the mountains. More often than not they would return after several weeks with just enough gold dust to survive on until the next job came along. One rancher even provided them with a grubstake from time to time in exchange for forty percent of the gold they located.

After a dozen years or so, they had come to be considered locals of Clermont, Colorado. Most of the town's folk could not quite remember a time when Red and Jim were not around. They had become local color, *real gold miners,* for the few tourists that stopped in town.

The other residents of Clermont found it quite amusing that their claim to fame, as a town, was a pair of grubstakers named Big Red and Little Jimbo. Occasionally a tourist would stop in the diner and ask where they could find Big Red and Little Jimbo. By mutual agreement, the tourist was always told the two miners could be found somewhere up in the high lonesome. It worked well for everyone, protecting the boys' privacy and satisfying the tourist that they really did exist.

They had made the adjustment and they had remained close friends. They found life in the thirties and forties quite interesting. After all, they knew what to expect. They knew about television and what it would become, before anyone else had even heard the word. They knew about World War II looming just ahead, before the name Adolph Hitler had any meaning to anyone at all. They knew what to expect and as interesting as that made life, it also made it a challenge. Biting their tongues had become something they had learned to do well.

Damon, who kept a close watch on the boys at first had grown comfortable with the boys' presence in a time before their own. Their handling of their situation pleased him greatly and bore out his deep-seated faith in the ultimate good of mankind. As the years wore on he checked on Red and Jim less and less often, directing his attentions to other matters of importance where his help was needed.

Malic had been raised to the status of Guardian and often joined Damon as he observed the boys' lives in Clermont. He, too, was proud of the two friends. He, more so than Damon, felt an attachment to Red and Jim. After all, they had taught him a lot about human nature and he had been delighted to no end, as he had learned first hand about them.

In 1966, Red got the notion that he would like to go back to Illinois and meet his parents as young people. Jim found the idea equally intriguing.

"Yeah, Red. That would be cool wouldn't it? I mean our parents would be about ten years old. They would have no idea who we are, would they? They haven't even met each other yet, let alone gotten married and had me. I could actually talk to my ten year old mom and dad! That's simply wild!" Jim stated, with great enthusiasm.

"It would be fantastic!" Red declared. "How many people get *that* opportunity? And—we wouldn't be breaking our promise to Malic either. They wouldn't know us from the neighbor down the street at ten years old. We wouldn't be revealing anything at all that could be considered altering the future or divulging any secrets. Not if we kept our mouths shut and just acted like a neighbor from the next block over," Red reasoned.

"And what would happen in 2037 as you each grow into manhood?" a familiar voice asked. "What would happen when your moms and dads began to realize that they had met their own children when they were children themselves? Two of your four parents do live that long. Do you think they would not remember? Do you think they would not recognize you as the neighbors who came to visit when they were ten years old?"

"Malic!" Red said, turning to see who had joined them unannounced at their camp.

"Yes, it is me, and what I have said is the reason you must drop this notion of visiting your parents as children. They *will* remember you as you grow older and become the men they met in their youth. Not you two specifically, but the children that will become you after they are born to them in 1981."

"Malic, sit down," Jim invited. "It's been so long and it is so good to see you."

"And it is good to talk with you again, but I am serious about abandoning this idea of yours. Damon and I have been very proud of you for your discretion in your new lives. We realize that you did not foresee the danger in this idea, so I came to warn you of its ramifications. Do you now understand?" Malic asked.

"Yes, I see it now," answered Jim. "But please, Malic, sit and join us for a while."

"Red, do you understand?" Malic asked.

"Yes, Malic, I do. We will stay here and drop the idea. Now, do as Jim asks and have a seat. It's been too long since we have talked. How have you been?"

Malic smiled and seated himself across from the boys.

"I have been well. I am now a Guardian. No longer just an aide. Damon and I have watched you over the years, more often at first, then less frequently as we grew comfortable with your adjustment to your new lives. You have done well and we are proud of you and the complete fulfillment of your promise to us."

"Sometimes it's hard, Malic. To keep the promise, I mean. There are times when we know things others might benefit from and we are bound by our word to let them suffer through without our help," Jim commented, lowering his eyes to the ground. "Sometimes it is damn hard, Malic."

"Yes, I know, but that is their life as it was intended to be. You are not at liberty to intervene. They have Guardian Angels to help them with their decisions and to watch over them. They also have the Guardians if they have earned our attention through their previous good deeds. Regardless, you are just visitors in their life spans. Please continue to remember that."

"We will, Malic. Will we ever be permitted to meet Damon?" Red asked, out of the blue.

"Would you wish that above all else?" Malic asked.

"It would be cool," Jim answered.

"Would you wish that above all else?" Malic repeated.

"I don't know, Malic," Jim answered.

"Red?" Malic asked.

"I don't know if I can say that either," Red answered.

"When you *can* answer that question, we will discuss it," Malic stated. "Until then, remember that he is watching over you."

Malic rose and smiled at each boy in turn.

"I must return to Ahveen now. I have duties to attend to," Malic said, dryly.

"Okay, Malic. It's been good seeing you again," Jim said, warmly.

"Yes, it has, Malic," Red confirmed.

Malic turned to leave, then stopped and spun back, facing the boys.

"And it has been good talking with you again," Malic said, sincerely and smiling at each of the boys. "Were I Kinder I would be proud to consider you my friends."

Malic turned again as Red responded to Malic's last comment.

"We're not Guardians or Olinians, but we consider you our friend, Malic."

Malic stopped momentarily and stood motionless. He was torn. He knew full well what lay ahead for the boys and wanted desperately to prepare them for it. But, that was forbidden. He had already put his request in to Damon for their salvation and there were still fifteen years left for Damon to consider his request. Malic wished deeply that Damon would not take all that time to arrive at his decision. He glanced a quick look back at the boys and smiled.

"Perhaps I worded that incorrectly," he said. "What I meant to say was that if I were Kinder I would be proud to live among you as your friend. I do already consider you each a friend."

Malic turned once more and became the bobcat once again, bounding off into the darkness. Red and Jim sat in silence, each wondering if they would ever see Malic again. There seemed something almost final in his voice as he had departed. They had no way of knowing.

※   ※   ※

As 1981 arrived, the boys, now men in their early seventies, were troubled by the fact that this was the year in which they were each born. Their lives, by all rights, should be just beginning this year, but they were growing into old men with each passing day. Somehow, their deal with Malic and Damon did not seem very equitable any more. They were feeling cheated, not out of chronological years, but out of the opportunity to live within those years they were intended to live within. The thought process was complex. There were so many thoughts to sort through. They *had* been given the opportunity to live years before their time, and they had been given the opportunity of seeing the future beyond their time. Also, they had witnessed history in the discovery of the Indian village, hundreds of years before their time. *So what wasn't fair?* they wondered. What they decided, together, was that they *could not decide* if their lives had been fulfilled. The question was just too complex.

As May arrived and the weather warmed, they decided that it was time, once again, to head into the mountains to prospect for gold. Prospecting had grown to be their favorite pastime. It took them into the most beautiful country, but more than that it took them away. It wasn't that they didn't like Clermont; they did. It was a wonderful town. It wasn't that they didn't like the townspeople; again, they did. They were a great community of hard working, God fearing people.

For Red, the need to get away from town stemmed from the knowledge that Laura would be born this year. That troubled him deeply. He had fallen in love with her, there was no getting around that, and after all these years he still loved her. The idea that she was now about to be born, a helpless infant, and he over seventy years old, was an unbearable thought to him.

Jim, on the other hand, had no such baggage to carry. His need to be away was borne of the image that had become indelibly imprinted in his mind. Every day that passed brought him one day closer to his birthday, his actual birthday. The vision stuck in his mind was of his parents bringing him home from the hospital and placing him in his crib, proud and delighted over their new son. He felt an extreme jealousy for this infant that would be lying in *his* crib. It should be him, the now him, not the next him, but then, they were one in the same.

It was a thought that he knew he could not dwell on for long without falling into a deep depression. He sensed that and tried to avoid thinking about it as best he could. The mountains seemed to help.

Malic saw their anguish also. He was deeply troubled by it, but powerless to help in matters such as this. *If Damon would only make his decision*, he thought. But every time he asked Damon, Damon would reply that it was ultimately up to Otheon and Otheon had not decided one way or the other as yet.

"Damon. Do you realize that Red's birthday is only five days away, and Jim's two weeks after that?" Malic asked.

"Yes, Malic. I am aware. I will go to Otheon again and plead your case once again. Perhaps today he will come to a decision. I'm not sure, but I imagine he has discussed it with the Father and there are probably concerns of which we are not aware. Remember, this situation has never arisen before. You must realize, Malic, that there is the matter of duplicate souls to be considered. *That* is a whole new concept, even in Heaven or Ahveen."

"Thank you, Damon. Please do what you can. I have grown fond of these two over the years, as you well know."

"I'll do my best for them, Malic. That I promise, but that is all I can promise."

On the morning of June 21 the boys struck pay dirt. In all their days of prospecting they had never seen anything like it. It was an appropriate birthday present for Red. The dry streambed they had traveled up many times before, gaining access to Eagle Peak, was now littered with nuggets and flakes of gold the likes of which they never dreamed existed. They sifted out the larger nuggets first and marveled at the number and purity of them.

"Damn, Red! This is one hell of a birthday present for you," Jim said, holding a double handful of one-ounce nuggets in his cupped palms.

"I'll say it is! Happy Birthday to me!" Red yelled.

"You know, Red. We better have a look upstream and see if we can determine where these nuggets washed down from."

They proceeded up the dry bed, picking up nuggets as they went and whooping and hollering all the while. It was a sight not easily described of two men in their early seventies acting like little boys on an Easter egg hunt. They pranced around and kicked up dirt, laughed and cried. Finally, thirty yards up the streambed, where the nuggets had grown as plentiful as sand on a beach, Jim stopped, gazing at the sight before him.

"Red. Look at that. Would you just look at that!" he marveled.

There, on the side of the streambed, where it had cut its path through solid rock forming a narrow canyon, was a vein of gold bearing quartz. Red reached out and literally plucked a nugget from the crumbling quartz ore.

"Damn! This is one rich vein," he commented to Jim, grinning from ear to ear. "But, you know, we've been through this cut before, lots of times. This vein wasn't exposed then and the bed was just so much rock and grit."

Jim thought about that for a minute, looking around, and replied, "You're right, but this canyon is deeper now than it used to be, buy ten or fifteen feet." He paused for a moment, looking up the forty-foot high wall of the cut. "Malic..." he whispered.

"What?" Red asked.

"Malic did this. He weathered this canyon by a few thousand years, somehow. That's why it's nearly twice as deep as it used to be—Malic did this! But—Why did he wait until we were seventy years old to make us rich. Why not back when we could have enjoyed it a while?"

Red was considering what Jim had just said when, as if a door had just been opened for him, he saw it clearly. He began to tell Jim what had just come to him, but Jim just stood staring at him, eyes wide and his body shuddering. Jim didn't seem to be able to hear him, so he yelled, but Jim only shuddered more heavily and his mouth gaped open as he took a step back. Red started to put his hands up to cup them around his mouth that he might be heard better by Jim, when he noticed his hands were translucent; nearly transparent. He placed them over his eyes and could still see Jim backing away from him. Then, he was in a dark place.

Jim could not believe what his eyes had just seen. He had stared at his lifelong friend in total disbelief as Red had slowly become transparent and then had slowly faded away like smoke. At one moment Red had appeared normal and the next had revealed the stream bank directly behind him. Jim had watched as Red had silently yelled to him, and had vanished from sight!

For a long moment Jim simply stared, motionless, expecting Red to rematerialize. Then, he screamed, "Red! Red! Oh my God, Red! Where are you? Come back!"

Jim fell to his side, curling up into a fetal position in the dry streambed. He cried like a baby for several minutes and then whimpering uncontrollably, rose to his feet.

"Malic! Malic! Please—Malic, what's happened to Red?" Jim cried to the winds.

❦   ❦   ❦

Malic was watching from his window. He turned to Red and said, "Go to him, Red. Explain to him. Make haste as he is in anguish."

Red took two steps toward the portal and became the bobcat. In a matter of a fraction of a second he was by Jim's side.

"Jim, I'm here," he said softly. "Don't despair, Malic has fixed everything."

"Red? Oh my God, Red, is that really you?" Jim asked, spinning in the direction of Red's voice. "Where did you go? I mean I saw you vanish before my eyes! I don't understand," Jim said, trying to collect his thoughts into something understandable.

"I was born, Jim."

"What?" Jim asked.

"I was born, in this time, just a few minutes ago. Remember what Malic told us years ago? 'Co-existence has no existence.' What he meant was that we, you and I, cannot exist in the same time as ourselves. I was born this morning at eleven forty five in Rockaway, Illinois. At that moment, as I drew my first breath, I ceased to exist here. You and I have only one soul each. It can't be shared with the new infants we are to become this year; that I have already become in Rockaway. Damon knew this, as did Malic. Otheon explained it to them, after he discussed our plight and us with the Father. It was decided that rather than let us fade into oblivion as our souls transferred to our newborn selves, that we would be given new souls and become residents of Ahveen. Malic, working through Damon, convinced Otheon and the Father to allow me to become a Guardian Aide, saving this me from oblivion. It's awesome, Jim! I actually turned into a bobcat to come tell you all this!"

"And—on my birthday?" Jim questioned.

"You'll join me, in the mountain. It's only two weeks away and we'll be watching over you until then. Malic and I. You'll be fine until then. Malic is your Guardian until then, then you'll become his aide."

"What about you, Red? Whose aide are you?" Jim asked, beginning to accept what he was being told.

"I'm Malic's aide right now, but time inside is different than out here. By the time you arrive, I'll be a Guardian."

Jim smiled at his old friend and laughed a roaring laugh as Red became the bobcat and loped away, flicking his stub of a tail as he went.

CHAPTER 13

The Completed Circle

*A*t Six o'clock Sunday morning, July 7, 2002, Jim Preston stared out his bedroom window to the street below. The streetlights still burned as the early morning sky had turned a deep royal blue and Rockaway, for the most part, still slept beneath it. Anxious for morning to arrive, sleep had eluded Jim for most of the night. *Today was the day.*

Red Porter had been Jim's best friend since before he could remember. They had gone to school together beginning in nursery school and continuing through high school. They had both graduated from Rockaway High three years ago, but neither had plans for college. Jim did remember a little about their friendship in kindergarten, but before that point in time he had only photos that his parents had taken to verify that they had been close ever since they were each two years old.

Jim had realized right away that he didn't really want to go into the Colorado wilderness alone and it would be much more fun if he had someone to share the adventure with. So, he had asked his best buddy and Red had jumped on the chance to go and hadn't stopped talking about it ever since. It took some serious talking to get their vacations at the same time, but, with a great deal of persistence, they had finally convinced Mr. Miller to see it their way. He had told them, "No way—before Independence Day", so they had had to wait until now.

♦   ♦   ♦

Although the restaurant was small, and old, it was busy. There were only two booths open so they took the corner booth next to the jukebox. Only two or three minutes passed before the waitress came to their table and greeted them warmly, smiling a dazzling smile at them.

"Hi fellas. What's it going to be tonight? The special is roast beef and gravy with your choice of any two sides."

"Hi Laura," Jim replied, reading the waitress's nametag. *Boy, she's pretty*, he thought.

"Yeah, hi," answered Red. "I'll try the special with a good hot cup of coffee, please. Mashed potatoes and creamed corn."

♦   ♦   ♦

"Excuse me," a voice said, from the next booth over. "Did I hear you boys mention the Cats' Lair?"

Jim turned and looked directly into the face of a very elderly man.

"I'm sorry. Harold Gillespie. Sorry to intrude," he added.

"No—that's okay, pleased to meet you. I'm Jim Preston, and this is my friend, Red Porter," Jim replied. "Yes. We mentioned the Cats' Lair. Have you heard of it?"

"Yes, but only once. I'd say it's a place to stay away from, if it exists."

"Why do you say that?" Jim asked, a little worried at Mr. Gillespie's comment.

"Well, I was just a boy, mind you, when I heard the name. I may never have remembered it at all if I hadn't seen with my own eyes what I saw. It was right here, in this diner, although it was called the Clermont Café back then, probably around 1930 or so. A fella, looked like a farmer to me, from Illinois or Indiana, forget which, came in asking questions about that place—your Cats' Lair place. Well, nobody had ever heard of it then, either, and the fella went off searching for it up on Father Mountain, or so he said he was going to do. He never came back."

⁂

"Okay then, what about Laura? Do we take her along? Laura—when could you leave if we decide to include you on this exploration?" Jim asked her.

"Tomorrow morning. I'll get my friend Alice to fill in for me here at the diner. She's always willing to earn a little extra since she retired from here last year. Would that be soon enough?"

"What do you say, Red? Yes or no?" Jim asked.

"I say okay. Let's do it! You and I can go see how far the roads will take us and how far a field your Jeep will take us tomorrow when we actually go looking. It'll give us one less day to search for the Lair, but it won't be a total waste of a day."

⁂

Red opened his eyes. Morning had arrived in Lynx Canyon and the first rays of sunlight were beginning to filter through the canvas of Laura's tent. He didn't remember dreaming at all during the night, but this night had been a dream come true in itself. Laura was sleeping peacefully by his side looking even more beautiful in sleep than when she was awake. Red took a deep breath and blew it slowly out through pursed lips. He nudged Laura's arm gently and waited for her eyes to open.

"Good morning," he whispered softly.

"Good morning, Red. Sleep well?" she asked.

"Never better," was his only reply.

"I guess we better get up and make sure Jim doesn't leave without us. He's chomping at the bit over finding the Lair and if we don't get out there we'll probably get left behind," Laura commented, smiling at Red.

Red smiled back and replied, "You've got that right!"

Laura leaned toward Red and gave him another little peck on the cheek.

"Come on, let's find that Lair," she said, and crawled out of the tent.

Red whispered, "Thanks," and followed her.

Of course, Jim was already up and sitting by the remnants of their fire, eating a can of cold beans. Between bites he was studying the valley in apparent consideration of where to begin his search.

"Hey, Jim," Red greeted. "Good morning."

"Good morning to you two, too. How'd you sleep?" he asked, winking at Jim.

"Great, thanks," Red replied.

"Laura?" Jim asked.

"Just fine, Jim. What *are* you eating?" she asked.

"Cold beans—They're great. I didn't feel like building a fire," he said, taking another bite. "I just want to get going. You guys grab something to eat so we can start our search—okay? I've been studying the valley and I think we should start on the other side of the lake, by the falls, where Laura has seen bobcats in the past. If nothing turns up there we can move along that side of the valley and circle back to here. Sound like a plan?"

"Sounds fine to me," Red answered.

"Me, too. Let's eat then and get moving," Laura said.

Laura opened her pack and pulled out a pecan coffee cake.

"Care to join me, Red?" she asked.

Red's eyes lit up.

"Sure! That looks great! It sure beats cold ravioli," he replied, plopping down on the ground beside her. "You're just full of surprises!"

They sat and talked and enjoyed their breakfasts for about a half hour before Jim could finally stand it no longer.

"You guys ready yet?" he asked, standing and dusting off the seat of his pants.

"I guess we better be," Red said, laughing. "Laura—you ready to go?"

"Ready."

"Okay then. Let's move out," Jim said, motioning toward the falls.

They gathered their packs, hiked them onto their backs, and headed out around the lake. They had no idea what awaited them on the other side, but they were anxious to find out. The Lair would be either a boon or a bust, *if* they found it at all. Part of the fun would be in the looking, but Jim, more than anyone else, hoped for much more.

As the trio rounded to the other side of the lake, Jim spotted someone sitting on a large rock by the shore, partially hidden by a small fir tree.

"Look, Red. Someone's there, by the shore," he pointed out.

Red looked to where Jim had pointed and saw him also.

"Yeah, I see him. Who the hell could that be?"

"I have no idea. I was under the impression that this place was rarely visited—by anyone," Jim commented, surprised at their seeing someone up here.

"Maybe he's a fisherman," Laura suggested.

"I don't see his pole. He appears to be just sitting and looking out at the lake," Red said.

They moved around in a circular path toward the person sitting on the rock, getting closer, but not walking directly toward him.

"Look," Jim said. "There are two people there."

From their new angle the kids could see that there was a second person sitting alongside the first they had seen earlier.

As the trio of young explorers tried to decide how to approach the two strangers, the two old prospectors were already discussing them.

"Remember, Jimbo. We can say whatever we want, truthful or deceitful, as long as it is in direct response to their questions," Big Red reminded Little Jimbo.

"I remember. Are you as nervous about this as I am?" Jimbo asked.

"Yes, I believe I probably am," Red answered. "It's not every day that you get to talk with your former selves."

"Or—to try to save them from themselves," Jimbo commented.

"True."

The kids decided to simply hail the two strangers when they came to within talking distance. They didn't want to startle the two men or alarm them needlessly by approaching too close at first. They moved toward them and stopped about twenty-five feet short.

"Hey! Hello!" Laura greeted.

They had decided a girl's voice would be less threatening.

"How's the fishing?" she asked.

The two men turned and looked over their shoulders at the kids, then spun about, slowly, to face them directly.

"We're not fishing," the elderly Red replied. "We're prospectors," he informed them. "Just taking a short rest before going back to our claim. It's peaceful up here by the lake. We come here often to relax."

"Well, I'm Red, and this is Jim and Laura," Red said, introducing themselves to the prospectors. "We're up here looking for a place called the Cats' Lair. Have you ever heard of it?"

"Sure," the elderly Jimbo answered.

"Is it close?" young Red asked.

"It was, when it still existed," answered his older self.

"Still existed?" Jim asked.

"Yes. The Cats' Lair was a large rock at the far end of the lake, on top of the cliff. It was an immense boulder, and bobcats could frequently be seen sunning themselves on it; hence, the name. This curious boulder was precariously perched on the top of the cliff by the headwaters of the waterfall, right at the brink of the north wall," The elder Jim explained. "I believe French fur traders first sighted it and gave it its name."

"What happened to it then?" Laura asked. "You keep saying that it *was* there. What happened to it?"

"There was a large earthquake in 1986, perhaps you remember it. It was centered near here and it shook this area violently, sending the Lair into the lake below," Big Red explained.

"Damn, then it's gone? For real?" Jim moaned.

"Yes, I am afraid it is unless you'd care to go diving to see it. By the way, if you don't mind my asking, how do you know of it? It wasn't something that many people knew about or even cared about all that much," Big Red questioned the group.

Jim pulled their map from his shirt pocket and handed it to him.

"I found this map, buried in a jar in Illinois," Jim explained. "I thought there might be something special about the Cats' Lair, or something. I don't know, but I got curious and Red and I came out here for a look for ourselves."

"Gee—Sorry to disappoint you fellas, but the only ones that have suffered from its topple into the lake are the bobcats. They lost their sunning spot," Big Red said, smiling. "Sorry you came all this way for nothing."

The elderly Red extended his arm and said, "Here's your map back."

"Keep it. I guess it's of no use to us anymore," young Jim said, looking up to where the old prospector said the Lair was once perched. "I know it wasn't anything special now, but damn, it would still have been neat to see it up there. Especially after driving and hiking all this way."

The two Guardians now had what they had come for. The map had been offered to them of the boys' own free will. Yes, they had lied, but that was all a part of protecting the portal. They had not impeded the boys' free will and that was all that was required of them. As it was now, they would never have to worry about another intruder in the portal. Caspeic, after all, had been retired from active duty some time ago. This was the only map and would remain the only map to the portal and its access.

Damon smiled as he watched through the window. His former trainees had done very well, perhaps even better than Malic might have done. His elation was shattered, however, as he saw the elder Red insist that the boys keep their map.

With the map still in hand, extended to Jim, the elder Red smiled at the younger Jim and spoke.

"Jim, keep your map, please. It will be a reminder of your adventure here when you grow old. You can tell your grandchildren about how you ventured all the way out to Colorado in quest of the Cats' Lair. It will make an interesting story, and—it will keep the memories of your youth alive, long after you have turned old and gray."

Jim reached over and took the map, placing it in his shirt pocket.

"Yeah, maybe you're right. My grandkids will probably get a kick out of the story and I'll have the map to show them. It'll make the story seem more real to them."

Damon was speechless. His mind raced at the incredulity of what he had just witnessed. Why?—Why in the name of all that's holy did his new Guardians just undo what they had worked so hard to accomplish? *Unbelievable!* he thought, almost blurting out the word, stopping short of a scream. He became the bobcat and bounded into the portal.

He reached Big Red and Little Jimbo halfway back to the Lair and confronted them.

"What in the name of the Father have you done?" he yelled. "Did I see what I thought I just saw? You returned the map that they had given of their own free will?"

Red smiled at Damon and shook his head.

"Damon—relax. Here is your map," he said, handing the folded paper to Damon.

"But—I saw…"

"You saw me hand them a map, but, not this map. Not Caspeic's map."

"But, then—what map?" Damon asked, confused for only the second time in his afterlife.

"Patience, Damon. Patience. You'll see all through the window in time," Red responded.

Red placed his hand on Damon's shoulder and turned him in the direction of the portal.

"All will be revealed—in time—Damon," Red repeated.

Damon turned back to the portal under the influence of Red's persuasion. They began to walk back, becoming the bobcats once again.

These boys, he thought to himself. *My newest Guardians…will surely be the challenge of my afterlife and the end of my peaceful existence!*

※　　　　　※　　　　　※

Having returned to their camp, Red, Jim, and Laura sat by the remnants of their previous night's fire. Each sat in silence and stared at the ground at their feet. Finally, after a long silence, Laura was the first to offer a thought.

"Red. Now that you know what the Lair really is, will you be going back to Illinois?"

"I don't know, Laura. I hadn't given it any thought. We are due back at work in a little over a week, but it's just a job. Nothing special. Why do you ask?"

"Because—I'd like it if you could stay out here with me. I know we've only just met and all—and you have a life back there—but, I was just hoping…"

She lowered her eyes to the ground and continued.

"I was just hoping that maybe you'd stay around a while and we could get to know each other better—that's all," she confessed.

Red sat silently. He looked at Laura and smiled, searching for the right words. He looked at Jim with uncertainty on his face, which Jim read instantly to mean that Red wanted his encouragement.

"Hell, Red. What've you got to go back to in Illinois? A dead end job pushing papers at the foundry? A lonely one-room efficiency? I say stay! The hell with Rockaway, and I'll stay, too. We can find jobs here and a place to live. Hell, we can be roommates…at least for a while," he said, smiling devilishly, and winking at Red and Laura. "I'm staying. Red—What's your decision?"

"I'm staying, too! Rockaway—see ya later!"

Laura's face lit up like a Roman candle and she rushed around the dying embers of their fire to give Red a big hug.

"Great!" she exclaimed. "I can talk to some of the business owners I know in town and get you both fixed up with jobs. I have a spare room at my place you guys can use, rent free, until you find a place of your own. This is awesome, Red! Thanks! You won't be sorry. You'll both love it here…you'll see!"

The kids spent the rest of the day around their camp. They talked about their futures together in Clermont and about each of their families, Laura's in the immediate area, and the boys' back in Illinois.

They talked about where they had gone to school and compared experiences from their pasts.

Jim and Red, particularly Red, were getting to know Laura and she was learning all about them. They had a lot to talk about and the day flew by into evening. They built a new campfire to warm their second night on Father Mountain and their little room was bathed in firelight and warmth. They talked until early morning before finally retiring, Jim in his tent and Laura and Red in theirs.

When they awoke to their second morning in Lynx Canyon, they were greeted by sunshine and clear blue skies. The Cats' Lair had all but been forgotten. Today was about exploring the valley for its beauty and serenity, and getting to know each other even better.

After a breakfast of pecan coffee cake and coffee, which Jim brewed in a pan, they set out to explore the near side of the lake. While Laura and Red were engrossed in each other, Jim was engrossed in everything he could see in the valley. He even found two arrowheads near the shore and speculated on the possibility of there having once been an Indian village somewhere nearby at some time in the past.

After a supper of hot beans and franks, the threesome decided to stay one more night and depart for Clermont in the morning. When morning arrived, they were ready to return to town, Laura to her job at the diner and Red and Jim to their new lives in Colorado.

As they crested the ridge, Red asked Jim for the map. Red unfolded the map, looking back one more time at where the Lair once rested atop the waterfall. He glanced down at the opened map and froze in confusion at what he saw.

"Jim, look at this," he said, almost in a whisper. "The map is different. It's in English and it's not of Father Mountain, either."

"What's it of?" Jim asked, a strange, perplexed look on his face.

"It says, 'Mount Oro' and 'dry stream bed'. Down here at the bottom it says, 'Big Red and Little Jimbo's Claim'. Is that supposed to be us?" he asked, bewildered by the names on the map.

"Sounds like us," Jim agreed.

Laura took the map from Red and studied it closely.

"Mount Oro, or Gold Mountain, is about thirty miles from here, just on the other side of Clermont. It was renamed years ago for two old prospectors that went up there in search of gold and never returned," she explained.

"Big Red and Little Jimbo?" Red asked her.

"Yes, that's what they were known by. It happened the year I was born, so I've only heard stories. That was twenty years ago."

Red looked at Laura and smiled.

"I think you have now more than just heard stories, Laura. I think you've met them. I think we all have," Red concluded.

Jim's conclusion ran deeper than that though. He had a strange feeling that Laura had met Big Red and Little Jimbo more than just once. He didn't understand it, but he had noticed a strange familiarity in the faces of the old prospectors that had given him the map—a very strange familiarity…

Epilogue

2004

"I now pronounce you man and wife. You may kiss the bride."

Red and Laura kissed and turned to face their guests seated in the first two rows of the Clermont Methodist Church. In attendance were Red's parents, Laura's parents, and Jim and his mother, who had driven out with Red's folks for the grand occasion. These were the guests seated in the first two rows.

The guests seated in the rafters were Big Red, Little Jimbo, and Malic, who watched the ceremony, unseen, from above the pipe organ. They were fluffed up like proud cocks over the event taking place below.

Everyone was pleased; so pleased that no one even remembered how the wedding had almost been cancelled earlier in the day. The minister, Reverend James Kay, who was to do the honors had fallen ill on that very morning. Clermont had only the one minister in residence, the Reverend Homer Wilson commuting each Sunday morning from the Presbytery in Denver to conduct services in the town's only other church. Getting him there on a Saturday evening would be next to impossible.

Just as the decision was about to be made to postpone the wedding for one week, Father Orlando from Cheyenne showed up in town, and walked into the Hummingbird for a bite to eat. Katie, the waitress on duty, saw his white collar and knowing the situation, asked him if he would consider conducting the ceremony. He happily agreed and Katie gave him a big hug and directions to the church, reminding him twice that the wedding was set for seven p.m. She then telephoned Laura to tell her that her day had been saved.

So, the wedding went off without a hitch, and as Laura stepped down the first riser toward her guests, she turned to thank Father Orlando.

"Thank you, Father Orlando," she whispered.

"You are very welcome, Laura, and please—call me Damon."

2011

"Mommy, Mommy! Where's Daddy?" Laurie asked, running into the kitchen obviously excited over something.

"He's at the mine with Uncle Jim, Laurie,—Why?" her mother asked. "What's wrong?" Laura asked, picking Laurie up and brushing her bangs back with her hand. She gave Laurie a kiss on her forehead.

"There's a big bobcat in our backyard!"

"Oh—that's probably just Big Red, honey. Don't worry," Laura said, comforting her daughter.

"Who's Big Red, Mommy?"

"Just a bobcat that comes around—Daddy named him Big Red."

"Why does he come *here*, Mommy?"

"I don't know, Laurie. He just does. I guess he likes your daddy. Daddy goes outside and talks to him and even pets him on the head. I guess Big Red likes that," Laura tried to explain, not really understanding it herself.

"How come I've never seen him before?" Laurie persisted.

"He usually comes late at night when you're asleep in bed," she explained to Laurie.

"Why did he come in the daytime now? Can we go outside and pet him?" Laurie asked, excited over the possibility.

"Well—We can go outside and *see* him, but we better not try to pet him without your daddy here," Laura explained. "He is a wild animal, Laurie, and he doesn't know us like he knows your daddy," she said, not knowing why she was even agreeing to go outside.

Laurie jumped up and down with the thought of going out to see Big Red, a real bobcat. Laura took her daughter's hand and slid open the glass door to the deck. They walked out together into the back yard and stopped halfway between the house and the bobcat.

"This is as close as we should get, Laurie. We can see him fine from here," Laura said, getting a little nervous as they had approached to within twenty feet of Big Red.

For a minute or so they stood and watched Big Red, the bobcat sitting and looking back at them. Suddenly, Laurie broke free from Laura's grip and bolted forward toward the cat, yelling, "Mommy! He talked to me!"

"Laurie! Stop!" her mother screamed, and began chasing after her.

Big Red turned and darted back into the forest, Laurie chasing after him and Laura in close pursuit behind her daughter. Suddenly, the bobcat stopped and looked back at Laurie. Laurie stopped also and her mother caught up to her and swept her up into her arms.

"Laurie, what were you doing? You *know* wild animals are dangerous! You could have been hurt, honey."

"It's okay, Mommy. He said we're safe now."

Laura smiled at her precious little Laurie and then heard a tremendous explosion behind her. An instant later the concussion from the blast nearly knocked her from her feet. She turned to discover the house engulfed in flames. She looked back toward the forest and Big Red was gone.

When Laura gained her composure she looked into her daughter's deep blue eyes and asked, "Laurie, what did the bobcat say to you before you chased him?"

"He said, 'Hi Laurie—follow me'. That's all, Mommy. I'm sorry."

"It's all right, Laurie...It's all right."

Laura sat on the ground, holding Laurie, and watched their new home burn. Her mind raced back to the lake on Father Mountain and to the two old prospectors, *Big Red* and Little Jimbo. They had provided them with the wealth to afford the life they now lived. She had always thought that Big Red had looked familiar, but now she saw the resemblance clearly, for the very first time.

"Thank you," she whispered, still not understanding. "Thank you…"

About the Author

C.H. FOERTMEYER was born in Cincinnati, Ohio in 1949 and again lives there, where he divides his time between web authoring, writing, and a full-time job.

Formally educated at New Mexico State University, Mr. Foertmeyer had the opportunity to travel the Rocky Mountains and the New Mexico deserts extensively, gaining insight into these areas he writes about.

Glossary

Ahveen	Home of the Guardians, located within Father Mountain
Damon	Second Guardian of Ahveen
Father, The	The Father
Guardian	An Earth based angel responsible for the well being of worthy Kinder
Heaven	Heaven
Kinder	The children of the Father in any world
Malic	Guardian Aide, aide to Damon
Olin	Malic's home planet before his afterlife
Otheon	Master Guardian, in charge of Ahveen and Earth's timekeeper

0-595-23778-9

Printed in the United States
5739